Freedom From Failure

Also by Sirshree

Spiritual Masterpieces- Self Realisation books for serious seekers

The Secret of Awakening
Answers that Awaken: Access the Source of Wisdom within You
100% Karma : Learn the Art of Concious Karma that Liberates
100% Wisdom : Wisdom that leads you to experience and be established in your true nature
You are Meditation : Discover Peace and Bliss Within
Essence of Devotion : From Devotee to Divinity
Dip into Oneness : Beyond Knower, Known and Knowing
The Unshaken Mind : Discovering the Purpose, Power and Potential of your mind
The Supreme Quest : Your search for the Truth ends there where you are
The Greatest Freedom : Discover the key to an Awakened Living

Self Help Treasures - Self Development books for success seekers

The Source of Health: The Key to Perfect Health Discovery
Inner Ninety Hidden Infinity : How to build your book of values
Inner 90 for Youth : The secret of reaching and staying at the peak of success
The Source for Youth : You have the power to change your life
Inner Magic : The Power of self-talk
Self Encounter : The Complete Path - Self Development to Self Realization
The Five Supreme Secrets of Life : Unveiling the Ways to Attain Wealth, Love and God
You are Not Lazy : A story of shifting from Laziness to Success
Freedom From Fear, Worry, Anger : How to be cool, calm and courageous

New Age Nuggets - Practical books on applied spirituality and self help

The Source : Power of Happy Thoughts
Secret of Happiness : Instant Happiness - Here and Now!
Excuse me God... : Fulfilling your wishes through the Power of Prayer and Seed of Faith
Help God to Help You : Whatever you do, do it with a smile
Ultimate Purpose of Success: Achieving Success in all five aspects of life
Celebrating Relationships : Bringing Love, Life, Laughter in Your Relations
Everything is a Game of Beliefs : Understanding is the Whole Thing

Profound Parables - Fiction books containing profound truths

Beyond Life : Conversations on Life After Death
The One Above : What if God was your neighbour?
The Warrior's Mirror : The Path To Peace
Master of Siddhartha: Revealing the Truth of Life and After-life
Put Stress to Rest : Utilizing Stress to Make Progress
The Source @ Work : A Story of Inspiration from Jeeodee

Freedom From Failure

7 SPIRITUAL SECRETS THAT TRANSFORM FAILURE INTO A BLESSING

Based on the teachings of
Sirshree

FREEDOM FROM FAILURE
7 Spiritual Secrets that Transform Failure into a Blessing
Based on the teachings of Sirshree

Copyright © Tejgyan Global Foundation
All Rights Reserved 2017

Tejgyan Global Foundation is a charitable organization
with its headquarters in Pune, India.

Published by WOW Publishings Pvt. Ltd., India

First edition: January 2017

Third reprint: June 2018

Copyrights are reserved with Tejgyan Global Foundation and publishing rights are vested exclusively with WOW Publishings Pvt. Ltd. This book is sold subject to the condition that it shall not by way of trade or otherwise, be lent, resold, hired out, or otherwise circulated without the publisher's prior written consent in any form of binding or cover other than that in which it is published and without a similar condition including this condition being imposed on the subsequent purchaser and without limiting the rights under copyright reserved above, no part of this publication may be reproduced, stored in or introduced into a retrieval system, or transmitted, in any form, or by any means, electronic, mechanical, photocopying, recording or otherwise, without the prior written permission of both the copyright owner and the above-mentioned publisher of this book. Any person who does any unauthorized act in relation to this publication may be liable to criminal prosecution and civil claims for damages.

*This book is dedicated
to those who rise like the phoenix
from the ashes of failure to create history.*

———

*This book is dedicated
to those who considered failure
simply a milestone in their journey.*

———

*This book is dedicated
to Failure
upon which great success is built.*

Contents

Preface
Fail Feel Fly   vii

SECTION I
7 SPIRITUAL SECRETS
TO UNDERSTAND & OVERCOME FAILURE

SPIRITUAL SECRET 1
Acceptance is a Miraculous Power   3

    Luminous Lives—Thomas Edison   16

SPIRITUAL SECRET 2
This is That What I Need   21

SPIRITUAL SECRET 3
Failure is a Blessing   30

    Luminous Lives—Walt Disney   43

SPIRITUAL SECRET 4
The World is An Arrangement   48

SPIRITUAL SECRET 5
Highest Choices Lead to Highest Success   59

    Luminous Lives—Maharshi Karve   67

SPIRITUAL SECRET 6
Fear of Failure Stops Your Progress　　　　　　　73

SPIRITUAL SECRET 7
Anything Negative is an Illusory Reality　　　　　82
    Luminous Lives—Nelson Mandela　　　　　　91

SECTION II

7 STEPS

TO SHIFT FROM FAILURE TO SUPREME SUCCESS

STEP 1
Voice of Faith　　　　　　　　　　　　　　　　97

STEP 2
Inspired Action　　　　　　　　　　　　　　　110
    Luminous Lives—Helen Keller　　　　　　　119

STEP 3
Capability　　　　　　　　　　　　　　　　　126

STEP 4
Learning　　　　　　　　　　　　　　　　　139
    Luminous Lives—Oprah Winfrey　　　　　　149

STEP 5
Qualities　　　　　　　　　　　　　　　　　154

STEP 6
Understanding　　　　　　　　　　　　　　170
    Luminous Lives—Swami Vivekananda　　　182

STEP 7
Final Success　　　　　　　　　　　　　　　188

Preface

FAIL FEEL FLY

If you are facing a failure or a setback, the good news is: It is temporary. Yes, *this too shall pass*. Even though it may feel like this situation or this feeling will never change, but change is the law of nature. So this phase is not permanent. You can achieve success even after encountering failure. If you don't believe it, answer one simple question: Is there anybody in the world who has achieved success without facing some setbacks and failures?

Anyone who has ever achieved great success has faced more number of failures than successes. Be it the President of America, Abraham Lincoln, or genius scientists like Edison or Einstein, or the phenomenal author of Harry Potter, J. K. Rowling. There are innumerable such examples. The only difference between a "failure" and these successful people is that they did not let failure pull them down. This is because they did not consider it as a "failure;" it was like a milestone or in fact a stepping stone on their path of success. They dusted themselves off and began working again until they achieved what they wanted.

You may wonder how they were able to do so. They were able to do it because *they believed they could*. A human being is the most beautiful and powerful creation of God. You are the only being in this world who can think, develop ideas, and implement them to create what you want. You are programmed for success. Even if you don't do anything, nature is automatically pushing you towards success. In fact, whatever is happening with you is occurring on the path of success. You are on that path every moment; even right now. Negativity is the only factor that derails you from this path—be it negative feelings, thoughts, words, or actions. Avoid this block and you will be back on track.

Remember, there is no difference between you and someone else you think is much more successful than you. The same life force and the same power is flowing within both. Therefore you do not need to feel inferior. Let us see how to find this conviction with the help of a little story.

A wise old man with a serene glow on his face was once travelling by ship. He was relaxing on the deck and reading a book. Suddenly the captain announced a storm and requested all passengers to return to their cabins. Everyone ran from the deck into their rooms. It was almost an hour by the time the storm had passed. The captain of the ship came out and walked past the deck to inspect the mast. He was surprised to see the old man still sitting on the deck. His book was drenched and so he had kept it aside and was calmly watching the sea.

The captain approached him and asked, "Sir, were you here all this time? Weren't you afraid of the waves that were flooding the deck?" The old man smiled and said, "Oh, yes! I was indeed afraid. I too ran and took shelter. While the others may have rushed into their cabins, I remained still and took shelter within myself!"

This is the best approach to failures too. Whenever you are facing any failure or setback and feeling disturbed, go within yourself. Close your eyes and start practicing any meditation you may have learnt, or you can simply focus in the area of your heart with eyes closed. Thoughts may come and go. Don't go behind them. Slowly you will move beyond your body-mind into a peaceful place, which is untouched by any storm or failure. Here you will experience your true essence. You will realize that you are not a limited little being struggling in this world. You are formless and limitless. You are a divine being, you are the Consciousness, the Universal Self, the Source—which is the creator of everything in this universe. Hence there is nothing that you cannot achieve and nothing that you cannot create.

In that state of clarity, you will also gain the insight that failure is not what you had perceived it to be. It is not something to be feared and dreaded. It has arrived with a definite purpose. It wants to shake you, awaken you, and push you towards realizing your greatest potential and becoming your supreme version. It will raise you higher to reach the pinnacle of success. It is indeed a blessing—albeit in a scary-looking disguise.

Along with this insight and experience, the 7 Spiritual Secrets revealed in this book will bring about a paradigm shift in your understanding of failure. Your mind will change and your heart will open. Negative feelings will give way to positive and even happy ones. You will then be ready to take the 7 Steps to become capable of achieving the heights of success. The 7 stories interspersed in between will inspire you to attain your highest potential. The stories of these luminous lives demonstrate that highly successful people consciously or unconsciously are aware of and apply these secrets and steps in their lives to face and overcome failure. With this wisdom and inspiration, you will be all set to fly in the limitless sky of possibilities.

This entire process of transformation can be summarized as: Fail-Feel-Fly: Whenever you fail, turn inward and feel and this will help you transcend the negative feeling. The seven secrets too will change your feeling. You can then fly towards ultimate success. And this is how a spiritual warrior is born, the one who achieves victory over failure with the help of the most powerful tool in the universe—spiritual wisdom. So, are you ready to become a spiritual warrior?

Let's proceed on this amazing journey of freedom from failure with the 'happy thought' that you are bound to succeed because SUCCESS IS YOUR NATURE.

* * *

SECTION I

7 Spiritual Secrets to Understand & Overcome Failure

Spiritual Secret 1

Acceptance is a Miraculous Power

*With the power of acceptance,
every failure is converted into a stepping stone
towards success.*

Failure is an opportunity for change. However, most of us do not readily accept change. We should be aware that change is the law of nature. Indeed, change is the only visible constant in life. Everything that occurs in our life, whether positive or negative, changes after a period of time. Nothing is permanent. The knowledge of this law gives us courage when we are going through failures and prevents us from becoming overly excited and carried away during times of success. In the beginning, change appears strange, and people would rather have things go on as they always have. If we become ready beforehand for the upcoming inevitable change, we will be better able to accept it, and hence be less troubled by it.

Changes can occur in your career, relationships, health, environment, or possessions. With the understanding that change is the law of the universe, we won't be so worried, distressed, or unhappy when changes occur in our life. Instead, we will think that if a particular thing has changed or if we have failed in something, then something new will take its place. We will get something new—new friends will be made, new relationships formed, we will get a new and better job, new industries will emerge, new and better things will be created. If this conviction arises, then change will become a cause for happiness rather than sorrow. You will find yourself saying, "The old (job, business, house, person) was good in its time; now that it is gone, something new will take its place. Perhaps it will be even better than the old one!"

People without this understanding torment themselves with questions that have no answers: "Why this failure? Why has this change occurred? When will this be over? Will I ever find anything that good again?" They make even the slightest change or smallest failure into a huge cause for concern. Therefore when changes or setbacks appear, we shouldn't jump to conclusions straightaway. You should catch yourself before you start imagining the worst as soon as there is even a hint of a setback or a change in your life. If you observe each change or failure with patience and forbearance, then all your worst fears will prove to be baseless. If you calmly consider all the information before making assumptions or decisions, then every change and setback will be acceptable by you and every decision will prove to be right. Further, like the autumn leaves that turn into a beautiful multicolored extravagance when they change, you will see change as a source of delight!

With this mindset, you will always be prepared for life's inevitable changes. Your attitude will be: "Change is beautiful; let's be prepared for any change that may come our way." This readiness will keep you optimistic and satisfied. With new changes, new constructive and creative activities will be accomplished. New work will create a new life; the new creation will in turn create an opportunity for a whole new level of consciousness.

Every decision that you have made in the past was apt, given your understanding, the information available, and the circumstances as you assessed them at the time. If the decision now appears to have been a bad one, it is only by virtue of hindsight; a clearer understanding of the factors influencing the outcome of that decision now makes it appear inappropriate. Therefore, there is no point in feeling guilty or blaming anyone for unexpected outcomes.

However, we should definitely rethink in order to assess what went wrong, so as to learn valuable lessons. Do a 'post-mortem' of the decision to benefit from any lessons learned, and then bury the past. Not because past is bad, but because past is dead. When we fall, there is no point in grumbling over why we fell. The best we can do is to get right up again, but not empty-handed. We should pick up valuable "lessons learned" before we move on.

Power of Acceptance

A successful person has the ability to accept every episode in life, positive or negative. This is not blind acceptance though; what makes a successful person stand apart is his wisdom behind this feeling of acceptance. With this wisdom, he stays at the summit of success all his life. With the power of acceptance, he converts every failure into a stepping stone towards success.

Acceptance can be of two types: 1) Acceptance with complete understanding, which transforms us and our attitude and 2) Acceptance due to helplessness; a reluctant acceptance. There is neither a feeling of acceptance nor understanding in the second type, and the person curses his fate throughout his life.

If you have the feeling of unacceptance in your mind, i.e. you are not able to accept some setback or failure, then stop and think whether you have some preconceived notion about what success or failure is. Are you looking at the failure through the lens of some false belief? How should you be really looking at it?

If you are seeing failure with the wrong outlook, you will never be able to accept it. It is time you flipped your outlook. It may be difficult in the beginning to accept things. But as your feeling becomes more and more positive, and you gain more wisdom, soon you will be able to accept things as they are.

Effect of acceptance in the journey of life

Look at little children when you take them along on a train journey. When the train pushes them forward, they too bend forward and when it pushes them backwards, they too bend backwards. They simply go along with the jolts of the train. They do not offer any kind of resistance to those movements. However, in the case of grownups, when the train pushes them forward, they press themselves backwards and when it pushes them backwards, they force themselves forward. This is what they do throughout their journey of life. They keep resisting and struggling all along. When grownups alight from the train after a long journey, they feel fatigued in spite of having done nothing at all. But the children immediately jump down and start running around at the station feeling as fresh and happy as ever.

Grownups wear themselves down by rejecting every tug and jolt in the whole journey. Hence, go through your journey of life with the feeling of acceptance, and you will be much happier.

In the journey of supreme success, how are you dealing with failures? Are you looking at them as roadblocks? Or are you pausing and asking yourself, "Okay, now that failure has appeared, can I accept it?" If your answer is "Yes, I can accept it," you will instantly feel better. Then you will be able to think through the failure with clarity. Whatever you do next will turn out to be the best and you will resume your journey of success with new zeal.

While using this technique of acceptance, some people may have questions like: "If everything is to be accepted, should we not improve upon our mistakes? Should we not attempt to succeed? And will I get success as soon as I accept things?"

Of course you have to put in efforts to achieve supreme success, but with both your hands. When you don't accept failure, it's like one of your hands is tied up behind your back and you are trying to solve a problem with only one hand. Not a very good idea. Common sense says that it is much easier to solve problems using both your hands. To convert failure into a ladder to success, you need to accept it first. As soon as you accept it, both your hands become free. If your mind asks "Why me?", explain to it, "I need to come out of this situation and hence I must accept it first." This is the right approach.

You should neither take up wrong means to achieve success nor fear failure and stop working. Once you accept failure, there is a radical change in the way you handle it—you do it powerfully, with an open mind, and with great ease. If your first step is wrong, all the subsequent ones may be wrong. That is why it is important to learn the technique of acceptance before you begin your efforts for supreme success.

How to accept?

The way to accept is through a simple question: "Can I accept this?" In life we come across many unwanted situations that in turn lead to misery. Even trivial situations or setbacks force us to retreat in our shell and make us very unhappy. To break out of that unhappiness, ask yourself, "Can I accept this?" "This" implies that which is making you unhappy. For instance, some setback or failure has occurred. Ask yourself, "Can I accept this?" ("this" means that setback or failure).

"Can I accept this?" is a mantra that can work wonders. Whenever any situation arises, you will find that your answer will be 'yes' in almost 100% cases of smaller incidents. It is only because you haven't asked yourself that you have become withdrawn and constricted. Now after repeating this mantra, you won't live a closed life anymore.

When you experience the benefit of this mantra in smaller incidents, you will find that in 99% of the average occurrences also, your answer will be 'yes'. Examples of average or medium occurrences are a small accident or someone insulting you, in which case you flinch at once. At that moment ask yourself, "He has insulted me; can I accept this?" You will find that in 99% of the cases, your answer will be 'yes'. Thereby you will be immediately liberated from that thought.

After the answer 'yes', many of your problems will be solved. Make a habit of asking yourself in every situation, "Can I accept this?" It may happen that something may go wrong as soon as you wake up in the morning, someone may have done some mischief, or you may hear the blaring of loud music from your neighboring room or house, or dogs may not stop barking at night. In any case, just ask yourself, "Can I accept this?" And if you are able to accept it, then you will say, "Let it continue. If the dogs are barking, let them bark, I am accepting it." With this acceptance, a feeling of relief will instantly flood through you.

It is possible that you may get a negative answer in some situation. In that case, give yourself some time, and after an interval, ask yourself the same question again. For instance, a failure has occurred and you are unable to understand it. You feel it is not acceptable and your answer is 'no'. Accept your 'no' for the time being. After some time, ask again, "Can I accept it now?" You will find that after some time an affirmative answer will begin to emerge. This is likely in some instances. A positive answer may not appear immediately, but after a few minutes or a few hours, you will get the answer as 'yes'. You will feel relieved at once.

However, even after trying repeatedly, if your answer is still, "No, I cannot accept this," in those cases you should accept your unacceptance as well. Let us understand this with some examples. If you feel, "I cannot tolerate to see this man's face," then ask yourself, "Can I accept my unacceptability?" If you are worried about a failure you have faced, and that worry is constantly eating you, just ask yourself, "Can I accept this worry?" Your answer will be, "Alright, so I am worried. I can accept this." In this way, when you accept your unacceptability, something new is created. You will be amazed by the results of acceptance when you accept your unacceptance by saying, "Ok, this is how I am. I have faults but this is fine with me. I accept this."

Let us see one more time at what you can do when you cannot accept something:

1. Try to accept the situation after some time.
2. Accept only some part of the situation. Accept bit by bit.
3. Accept only the negative feeling that the situation is causing by identifying the feeling.
4. Accept not being able to accept it. This is a very critical step. Ask yourself, "Can I accept my unacceptance?"

How does acceptance work?

One of the principles of life is: What is true at one level is true at all levels. As in small, so in big. When you accept even a minor failure, then you have released your negative feelings associated with it. You may think that it is just a small step. But the fact is that it causes a giant shift in your consciousness. At that very moment, a lot of related and similar issues too get automatically accepted by your mind. As a result, you begin to attract success and everything positive towards you.

Thus, the smallest letting go action helps you in every facet of your life. Not only do you become mentally free, but it affects you at the physical, emotional, social, financial, and spiritual levels, and sets off a chain reaction that reverberates through your entire being, taking you to quite a different place than you were before. The moment you let go of the negative feeling through acceptance, you are telling your subconscious mind: "I am free from the feeling of failure. I am now open to the goodness and abundance of the universe. I want highest success and I'm ready for it."

How do you use this knowledge that even a small act of acceptance causes a giant shift in your consciousness? Simple. Whenever you find yourself troubled by a huge problem, accept something small—either related to the problem or not. This small shift will help you tackle the bigger one too.

You need to transcend past failures too. If you have truly accepted failure, it will remain only as a learning in your mind. There will be no baggage of emotions associated with it.

Why accepting works?

Acceptance works because it changes your mindset instantly. When we face a failure, it immediately generates negative feelings. We attempt to somehow get out of it as quickly as possible. But whatever we do, standing on the platform of negative feelings will not work. Actions based on negative feelings only make the situation worse. When things don't work, we think that taking more actions will solve the problem. Or maybe blaming someone else will. This simply results in further complications. What could have been done easily and effortlessly becomes a huge tidal wave of effort that does not yield any result.

There are many who go for a job interview, though they have a job in hand. They do it just to find their market value. The same people report that if for some reason they lose their job and then go for an interview, they usually make a mess out of the interview. They stutter or stammer their way through. Why? This is because the second interview is given standing on the platform of negative feelings of fear, worry, or insecurity. It only generates negative energy all the more.

When we accept the situation, this negative platform is demolished. The vortex of negative energy does not arise. In addition, we experience mental clarity. New avenues that were not visible earlier now become visible. Learners of a new language usually go through an important step before they become fluent in what they are attempting. They tell themselves it is alright to make mistakes. The moment they do this, they become bolder and better in the new language. If they haven't undergone this step, then they just focus on mistakes. The more they focus on mistakes, the more mistakes they make. Accepting stops this over-pushing and focusing on the negative.

The moment you accept the situation, it helps you in the following ways:

1. Built in negative energy dissipates.
2. Your focus changes from "what is wrong" to "what can be improved now."
3. The mind becomes clearer and calmer.
4. You become more single minded and focused. Other distractions diminish.
5. You see new avenues not visible earlier. The fog on the overall picture dissipates.
6. Your decision making ability is enhanced.
7. You feel more balanced emotionally.

8. Your irritation fades away or you get relief from a disturbed state of mind.

9. You unconsciously begin to reframe the words. What was irritating is now just a small botheration. Thus, your experience of life changes.

10. You feel freer to handle the situation at hand without the extra emotional and mental baggage.

11. The energy that was being consumed by your feelings of fear, worry, or anger is conserved. Thus, you have this extra energy at your disposal, which you can use for solving the given situation with renewed vigor as well as for other constructive purposes.

Acceptance does not mean running away from the situation

Many people think that accepting failure is as good as running away from the problem. But, acceptance is not fleeing from a situation; it is flying over a situation. You will be able to fly, because the moment you accept, you liberate yourself from the grip of negative energy.

Also, acceptance does not imply that you should stop having any wishes or stop the journey of supreme success. In fact, the journey of supreme success gives you a direction. If you fail to reach your planned milestones for some reason, then instead of abandoning your quest, you need to accept the situation. As soon as you do this, you are able to discover newer and innovative methods to reach your goal. This keeps alive your chances of attaining highest success. It helps you to not quit the goal altogether. Not accepting the situation can mean that you may choose the wrong path or maybe even stop your journey.

The Bhagwad Gita tells us about dispassionate action. Most people question how to be dispassionate. Acceptance does precisely that. It stops you from being too emotionally attached to your aim.

Acceptance moves you from yearning for your aim to focusing on your aim. It moves you from forcing yourself to freeing yourself so that you can take best actions for the situation. Suppose you want to go to sleep at night. If you force yourself to sleep, it's difficult to drift into sleep. Instead you tell yourself, "It's okay if I don't sleep. Can I accept that I am not able to sleep?" The moment you stop resisting it, you will fall asleep.

An important law of life is that whatever you resist shall persist. If you are resisting your failure, it will persist. When you resist the negative outcome, you actually focus on the negative and attract the negative. When you accept the negative, you no longer resist it and are free from it. Thus, accepting is not about running away from the outcome but about choosing a new outcome or a new avenue for an outcome because you are no longer constrained by negative energy caused by resisting, forcing, or yearning.

How do you know you have accepted?

In chemistry, a litmus test is used to decide whether a solution is acidic or not. Similarly, is there any such test that can tell you whether your acceptance was successful or not? There is. When you have accepted something, the setback or situation seems different. So, how do you apply the litmus test? Simple. After having accepted, review the situation in your mind. Look at the failure or problem again. If your acceptance has worked, (it usually does), then the failure or problem seems lighter and clearer. If there is still some negative emotion left over, again accept by asking, "Can I accept this?" Again look at the failure or situation in your mind. Has it lightened? Keep doing so till you are fully clear.

Instead of using, "Can I accept this?", you could also use the question, "How can I convert this failure into a ladder?" This too results in instantly releasing negative blockages. You will gain something from the failure, instead of losing something due to it.

In this way you begin to look at a failure or setback from a positive point of view. If you are looking at a failure positively, then how is it a "failure"? This understanding will shift your view permanently about "failures" of life and their purpose. This shift will make you feel happy instead of miserable on encountering any failures henceforth in your life. Because now you know what to do.

SUMMARY:

1. Change is the law of nature. Nothing is permanent. The knowledge of this law gives us courage when we are going through failures.

2. If you observe each change or failure with patience and forbearance, then all your worst fears will prove to be baseless. You will see change as a source of delight!

3. With new changes, new constructive and creative activities will be accomplished. New work will create a new life; the new creation will in turn create an opportunity for a whole new level of consciousness.

4. A successful person has the ability to accept every episode in life, positive or negative. With the power of acceptance, he converts every failure into a stepping stone towards success.

5. If you are unable to accept some setback or failure, then stop and think: Are you looking at it through the lens of some false belief?

6. When you don't accept failure, it's like one of your hands is tied up behind your back and you are trying to solve a problem with only one hand.

7. To convert failure into a ladder to success, you need to accept it first. Once you accept it, there is a radical change in the way

you handle the failure—you do it powerfully, with an open mind, and with great ease.

8. When you resist anything, you actually focus on it and attract it to yourself once again.

9. Acceptance is not fleeing from a situation; it is flying over a situation. The way to accept is through a simple question: "Can I accept this?"

10. Acceptance works because it changes your mindset instantly. The smallest letting go action causes a giant shift in your consciousness and helps you in every facet of your life. You begin to attract success and everything good into your life.

* * *

Luminous Lives

THOMAS EDISON

> *"I have not failed.
> I've just found 10,000 ways that won't work."*
> — Thomas Edison

Some people get dejected by failure, while some rise like the phoenix from the ashes of failure to create history. Their name is etched in golden letters in the pages of history. The most prolific American scientist Thomas Alva Edison is the best example in this context.

Edison considered every failure as merely a speed bump on his path of success. For instance, he faced constant setbacks yet continued to work relentlessly in order to develop a long-lasting, practical electric bulb. He spent an unbelievable amount of time, effort, and money in trying various materials from around the world to find the perfect material for the filament. When one material failed, he moved onto another, day after day and year after year, with almost 10,000 experiments. Yet he said, "I have not failed 10,000 times. I have not failed once. I have succeeded in proving that those 10,000 ways will not work. When I have eliminated the ways that will not work, I will find the way that will work."

And indeed he did. Edison lit up the world with his bulb. It is due to his perseverance and hard work that he made such inventions without which it is hard to imagine our present life, such as the commercially viable light bulb, the electric power distribution network, sound recording (phonograph), alkaline storage battery, motion picture camera, improved telephone, and so on. There are a total of 1093 patents in his name in the U.S. and many more in other countries, which are the most patents granted to any inventor in his time.

Younger years

Edison was born to an American family on February 11, 1847, in Milan, Ohio, United States. His father was a businessman and his mother had earlier been a teacher. He attended school for hardly three months and the results were not encouraging—his mother being outraged upon hearing that the teacher had spoken of him as "addled" or stupid because he was prone to distraction and was hyperactive. Edison's mother believed him to be receptive and thoughtful. She pulled him out of school and educated him at home better than what was possible in the local schools of the day. He showed a voracious appetite for knowledge, reading books on a wide range of subjects. In this wide-open curriculum Edison developed a process for self-education and learning independently that would serve him throughout his life.

He read every book within reach and tried every experiment that he read in science books. There is an incident where he induced a lad employed in his family to swallow a large quantity of Seidlitz powders in the belief that the gases generated would enable him to fly. The agony of his victim resulted in punishment from his mother. But he was not discouraged. Young Thomas at the age of 11 or 12, created his first laboratory in the cellar of his house. He spent all his spare time and pocket money on this laboratory without concern for food or play.

Early career

When his pocket money was not enough for his scientific endeavors, he first sold vegetables from his family farm and then started selling newspaper in trains. After some time, he started writing articles and news, and printed his own newspaper on the printing press that he established in the empty luggage compartment of a train. He also set up his laboratory in the compartment. Once due to jolts of the train, a fire mishap occurred in his lab. The furious rail conductor struck him on the side of his head and threw him out along with his laboratory and press. Due to this hard slap, his hearing power was compromised.

Although tearful and indignant on being thrown out of the train, Edison did not give up. He soon reconstituted his lab and printing press at home, and again prospered in his enterprise. One day he saved the station master's little son from being run over by a train. The grateful father rewarded him by teaching him to operate a telegraph. By age 15, Edison had learned enough to be employed as a telegraph operator. In his spare time, he read widely, studied and experimented with telegraph technology, and became familiar with electrical science. He improved upon the existing telegraphic devices and worked very hard to rise to the position of first-class operator. He said that his deafness in one ear, in fact, proved to be a boon in his career and some of his inventions.

Becoming a legendary inventor and entrepreneur

Edison moved to Boston for work, and in his spare time invented the electronic voting recorder, but nobody wanted his invention. He resolved to henceforth devote his inventive faculties only to things for which there was a genuine demand, something that catered to the actual necessities of humanity.

Barely 21 years old, he moved to New York and had no money even for food. After having requested a free cup of tea from a street vendor, he was wandering the streets. Coincidently the stock ticker machine of the Gold Indicator Company malfunctioned and crashed. This machine was used to send the quotations to businessmen by brokers. Edison repaired the machine and he was made in-charge of the whole plant the very next day.

In 1869, he invented the Universal Stock Printer, which synchronized several stock tickers' transactions. He was paid $40,000 for its rights. Edison was only 22 years old.

After having made some successful innovations, Edison devoted his full time to inventing and started an industrial laboratory and a string of companies. In the following years he became a renowned inventor and entrepreneur.

His inventions were not limited to one field but to various fields such as movies, sound recording, battery for electric cars, commercially available x-ray machine (fluoroscope), mining, concrete, rubber, producing air in submarines, and whatever was needed by people. He was one of the first inventors to apply the principles of mass production and large-scale teamwork to the process of invention, and because of that, he is often credited with the creation of the first industrial research laboratory. He was indefatigable, slept only a few hours, worked endlessly, and also pushed his employees to do the same. He always said, "Genius is one percent inspiration and ninety-nine per cent perspiration."

Edison firmly believed, "Many of life's failures are people who did not realize how close they were to success when they gave up." That is why he never wasted time in lamenting over failures but instead moved on with double the zeal and dedication until he accomplished his goal. This is how he succeeded in making more than a thousand inventions and literally changing the world.

He did not get upset by the ups and downs of life. On December 9, 1914, a massive explosion occurred in West Orange, New Jersey. Ten buildings in Edison's plant were wiped out. In spite of efforts to salvage as much as possible, many priceless prototypes and records were lost in the flames. The financial loss was estimated in millions of dollars. However, Edison accepted it with grace. While watching the fire, Edison calmly walked over to his distressed son and said, "Go get your mother and all her friends. They'll never see a fire like this again." Later, at the scene of the blaze, Edison was quoted in *The New York Times* as saying, "Although I am over 67 years old, I'll start all over again tomorrow."

And he did. The next morning, he looked at the ruins and said, "There is great value in disaster. All our mistakes are burned up. Thank God we can start anew." Such incredible attitude! He rebuilt his plant and continued successfully with his production and inventions till the end of his life. A truly luminous life.

• • •

Spiritual Secret 2

THIS IS THAT WHAT I NEED

Whenever and whatever you get in your life is your necessity. What comes to you is exactly what you need.

In the first secret, we learned about the importance of acceptance. The second spiritual secret goes a step further. It is a very profound secret. Let us understand it with the help of some examples.

Suppose you are not satisfied with your current job. You are praying, "O God! Give me a bigger, better job." After some days, your boss fires you. You are shocked; you prayed for a better job and lost even your present job. You consider it as a big failure. You lose faith in your prayer. You then start searching for another job and find there is a vacancy at a good firm and they are willing to hire only those who are currently not employed anywhere else! Thus, being fired from your old job was your necessity, otherwise how could you have got the bigger, better job? *The first scene was the preparation for the next scene.* Thus, in every situation, the truth is: "This is That what I need."

A little boy is going someplace. There are various paths which are winding and meandering. He is going on the wrong path and in the wrong direction in a maze from where there is no way out. A mysterious hand comes out of nowhere and gives a little smack on his head and points out: "There, there." He is astounded, frightened, and irritated at the same time. The hand smacks and points out at every turn. When he is being smacked, he is unable to say, "This is That what I need." But when he comes out in the right direction, he realizes, "Oh! All those smacks were to lead me to my destination." While being smacked if you had asked him whether he felt it was what he needed, he would have never agreed.

Once there was a man who built a beautiful bungalow with all his lifetime earnings. His entire family was very happy as they were going to shift to their new bungalow the next day. All the packing was done and everybody was chatting excitedly over dinner. And then the news arrived that the building of their new bungalow has collapsed! To everyone's astonishment, the next day the man was happily distributing sweets in his neighborhood. People asked him, why was he celebrating when he had suffered such a great loss?! The man replied, "I am so thankful that the building collapsed a day before we shifted there. My family is saved!" Thereafter, in order to lay a stronger foundation for building a new bungalow in its place, he got the laborers to start digging the place. While digging, a treasure was found! With the treasure, not only was his loss recovered but he also had much more in surplus.

If you conduct a survey to check how many people on Earth had accepted when something happened to them that it was exactly what they needed, you would hardly find any. They wouldn't have accepted since an understanding is required to accept it. One needs courage to accept the Truth (which comes through understanding) and to walk the path of Truth, as Truth is illogical. It does not seem to be correct and the mind does not accept it. What then should the mind be told? Let us assume that a situation arises where somebody steals your idea and touts it as his own. That person gets full credit for it and consequent fame and success. At such time, would you be able to say, "This is That what I need"? You won't, since your mind will say, "I simply cannot accept that this is what I need." This is because you are not aware of the next scene that would happen in the future. The truth is that whatever is happening with us at this moment is for our growth and progress.

We don't have to agree; we have to just know the secret

The body-mind in which thoughts are being produced has a particular quality: it has receptivity—receptivity for new ideas and thoughts. Thoughts pass through the body-mind; body-minds don't generate thoughts. Thoughts are coming from all sides. Thoughts see which body-minds are transparent and deceit-free, which have become eligible, which have become capable, and then enter those body-minds.

This is just a way of explaining something which is beyond words. Actually the Source of all thoughts, ideas, and feelings is within us and we are within it. Just like fish in an ocean. The same water is present inside the fish as well as outside. Likewise, the ocean of Consciousness, the Self, the Source is present all around us and is all-pervading. Ideas arise from the Source and then pass through only those body-minds that have become eligible for them.

When the person whose idea got stolen has this higher knowledge, he would be able to say, "This is That what I need." This is because he knows, "The source of thoughts and ideas cannot be stolen. With receptivity, I can get even better and higher ideas." Hence he will not be distressed by this situation. The mind will say, "I don't agree." Then you have to tell your mind, "It's okay if you agree or not, just know it." You don't have to agree, you don't have to disagree. But it's important to know it, because once you know this truth or this secret, then there is no necessity to agree. When we don't know it or don't understand it, then we have to agree because we have to begin somewhere. Therefore, the mind has to be told, "Don't get stuck in this cycle of agreement and disagreement, instead just understand that this *is* the truth. Become aware at least when the next scene appears. Earlier when the event was taking place you couldn't understand; when you were stuck in the maze you couldn't understand, when you were being smacked you couldn't understand. But at least now that you are out of it, start contemplating on it."

The mind has to develop this habit of contemplating on the truth and on all the secrets of life before the next scene appears. Tell yourself not to get into the complication of whether to believe or not, it is crucial to just know it. Understand that whenever and whatever you need, you get it. This means that whatever is happening to you now is your need and necessity. It may not be necessary for someone else, but it is definitely necessary for you.

Using common sense

We have to make use of our common sense when applying anything in our life. Suppose you lost some object, and you reminded yourself the mantra, "This is That what I need." After saying this mantra, it's not like you don't have to search for the object. You will definitely take corrective action and put in all those efforts that are necessary on your part. You will give the appropriate response to the situation. But on saying the mantra within, a feeling of acceptance permeates your being. Thereafter whatever will be done will be with all your intelligence and presence of mind. Otherwise, a brain loaded with stress cannot even think. Therefore you have to understand the meaning of what is being told and also how to apply it using common sense.

This secret does not imply that you have to accept the situation as your need and then do nothing. This has been happening in spirituality. When people are told one thing, they hold on to something different. Those who don't want to study, those who don't want to work, will find some excuse. Thinking themselves to be wise, they use words of wisdom to support their tendency of laziness and other vices. Avoid using these spiritual secrets as an excuse.

Understand the secret of prayer

When you say, "This is That what I need," the resistance in your feelings is released. This then helps in aligning your thoughts peacefully with what actions need to be taken next. It also helps you to see that what you were resisting is probably something you had yourself wanted.

Suppose you are waiting for the elevator to arrive and it's taking its own sweet time. First you will say, "This is That what I need." Your mind will relax. Then, until the elevator arrives, what will you do? Just ask yourself what you had prayed for. Someone prays, "O God! Give me patience," and the elevator does not arrive, or he has to wait in a long queue—be it at the bank, at the airport, at a store check-out, or wherever. He does not realize that this is the fruit of his prayer. If you want to develop patience, certain events will occur for making you patient. Otherwise, what do you expect to happen when you pray for patience? Will flowers or stardust be showered on you from the heavens and you will develop patience in an instant? That's not how it works. Such things are told in stories just to help children understand certain things.

Imagine you are going someplace and there is a traffic jam or the road is blocked. How irritated you could get! And when someone overtakes you from the side, how you feel like cursing them! But now that you know this secret, you would say, "This is that what I need. This incident has occurred to teach me something." Later on if you happen to meet that person who overtook you on the road ahead, you may thank him because he gave you an opportunity to apply your understanding of this secret and develop patience in you. It is not necessary that he understands why you have thanked him. At the least you can thank him in your mind immediately after the incident.

Thus, henceforth whenever you are waiting in a queue or waiting for anything else, or someone *tries your patience*, tell yourself, "I have prayed for patience. This is the opportunity arranged for me to practice patience." In what a beautiful manner your prayers are being fulfilled!

If you are praying, "Dear God! I need courage," then what will happen in your life? Particular incidents will occur as opportunities to help you practice being courageous. Perhaps someone will come and frighten you. In such a situation, you will say, "This incident will help me develop courage. This is That what I need." When you will get this thought, you will take up that situation as a challenge and soon you will find that you have cultivated the courage that you desired. But if at that time you have forgotten this secret, you will feel miserable.

Suppose you had prayed for supreme success, and then some difficulties and failures arrive. You would say, "This is That what I need." Your negative feelings will be released at once. You will then be able to think clearly and realize that this is the fruit of your prayer. You wanted supreme success, and these setbacks have arrived to make you strong, courageous, creative, and develop your skills, so as to make you capable of attaining supreme success. But if someone does not know this secret of prayer, and straightaway you tell him that whatever is happening is the answer to his own prayers, he may get very upset with you. Hence it is essential to have the knowledge of such spiritual secrets, so that you can apply them for your highest benefit. Just imagine how a person's life would be if he knows all the secrets of life? For the one who knows all the secrets and is fully convinced about them, how would he be living his life? It would be a life full of conviction and happiness.

Thus, use the mantra, "This is that what I need" for every failure or setback to understand that what you term as "failure" is not failure at all, and move ahead towards your goal with joy and faith in life and its secrets.

SUMMARY:

1. Whenever and whatever you get in your life is your necessity. Remember the mantra, "This is That what I need."
2. Every scene is the preparation for the next scene.
3. All the smacks that we receive in life are to lead us in the right direction towards our destination.
4. One needs courage to accept the Truth and to walk the path of Truth, as Truth is illogical.
5. The Truth is that whatever is happening with us at this moment is for our growth and progress.
6. The source of thoughts and ideas cannot be stolen. With receptivity, you can receive the best and highest ideas.
7. It does not matter whether the mind agrees or not, the important thing is it should know this truth.
8. After saying the mantra, you need to take corrective action and put in all those efforts that are necessary on your part. But on saying the mantra, a feeling of acceptance permeates your being, and thereafter whatever will be done will be with all your intelligence and presence of mind.
9. If you want to develop patience or courage, certain events will occur for making you patient or courageous.

10. If you want supreme success, and then some setbacks or failures arrive, their purpose is to make you strong, courageous, creative, and develop your skills, so as to make you capable of supreme success.

* * *

> "Failure is simply the opportunity to begin again,
> this time more intelligently."
>
> – Henry Ford

VOICE OF FAITH

TO SHIFT FROM FAILURE TO SUCCESS

Nature has bestowed me the understanding to overcome every problem.

I want to go through every experience without feeling disturbed.

I am full of enthusiasm and energy.

I am Complete. Every action is completed by me on time.

I am anchored in the heart of life.

Whatever I experience, I accept it from the heart.

Spiritual Secret 3

FAILURE IS A BLESSING

*To consider any event in your life as a failure
is the only failure.*

Our life is made up of events, which are sometimes according to our expectations and sometimes against our expectations. We feel happy if things turn out our way and unhappy if they don't. If we use the word 'failure' for events that have not shaped up as we expected, then the problem begins with this word itself. Instead of the word 'failure' if we say the words, "The incident that is taking place has a solution, a gift, a ladder, a lesson, and a challenge. This incident has come to give me a challenge… it has come to impart a lesson… it has come to become a medium or a ladder for my progress… it has come to give me a solution and a gift," then we won't feel that incident to be a failure. This is the third spiritual secret that every failure is indeed a blessing, albeit in a disguised form. This may seem radical and unbelievable at first. Hence let us delve deep into this matter to unveil the real form and purpose of failure.

Every failure contains its solution

The solution to a problem lies within the problem itself. The answer to a question lies within the question itself. You may wonder how this is possible. Some examples will help to clarify this very important point.

Diamond is one of the hardest material on Earth, and cutting it was a major problem. The solution was found in the diamond itself. A diamond saw made of diamond dust was (and still is) used to cut diamonds. Similarly, you may have heard that poison cures poison. Also, vaccines are made from the same organism that they are supposed to protect from.

Another kind of example is that when someone is unable to digest a particular fruit, the solution lies in the fruit itself. Supposing after eating a watermelon, one feels uneasy or unwell, then chewing 5-6 watermelon seeds will solve this problem. If one is unable to digest a fruit without its peel, say a guava, then it should be eaten along with its peel. Likewise, if a fruit causes problems with the peel, then it should be eaten after peeling.

Let us look at one more example. A person was traveling in a car and its tyre got punctured. He stopped on the side, removed the four nuts of the tyre and kept them aside. By chance these nuts fell into the drainage flowing along the edge of the road. Now this was a major problem. He did not know what to do. A young boy passing by asked him, "What happened? Can I help you?" The man looked at the boy and did not feel that this boy could help him. Nevertheless, he explained his situation. The boy said, "No big deal! Just remove one nut from each of the remaining three tyres and use them to fasten the spare tyre. In this way your car will safely reach a mechanic's workshop at least." The man was taken aback. The solution was so simple. It did not require a highly developed intellect, just some common sense. Thus, the problem came from the car and so did the solution.

These were some examples to demonstrate what is the problem and what can be its solution because quite often common sense plays a major role in finding the solution. Many a time great scientists fail to find a simple solution, whereas an ordinary person unknowingly ends up making a great discovery.

If you are facing a failure or a setback, you may be wondering how the solution lies within the problem, how the answer lies within the question? But this is a fact. It has been seen that many students do not read questions attentively and end up writing the wrong answers. Then they wonder why they got low scores. In most cases, the solution emerges as soon as the problem is correctly understood. Therefore each one of us has to understand how to look at a problem correctly. Proper analysis of the problem will bring forth the exact cause or obstacle, which can then be worked upon to solve the problem.

'Every problem has the solution within itself' is a profound secret of life which is continuously operating, whether one believes it or not. If you put your hand in fire, the law of nature states that the hand will get burnt, and it does. If someone says that they don't believe this law, they will be told, "Fine. Don't believe it. But the law still operates." There are laws of life, some known and some unknown, which are at work. Some people believe them and some do not. We have to neither believe nor disbelieve; we simply have to know them.

Crime detectives know that in order to catch the criminal they first need to get to the crime scene. Because that is where the clues are found and often the criminal too returns to the scene of the crime. These detectives know this law of life and hence they find solutions many a time at the crime scene.

Through various examples it has been conveyed how the solution is present within the problem. Tomorrow if you are confronted with any setback or failure, do not get tensed at once. Stop for a while, calm your mind, and see whether a solution can emerge from within the failure. When you think in this manner you will be amazed.

In the beginning it will be difficult to understand this and find a solution that may be very subtle. But as your faith increases, this fact will begin to manifest before you. This law plays a big role in your life.

From a higher perspective, to search for the solution of a problem is not the true solution. The true solution is that *you need to make space for the solution to emerge.* When you are disturbed by a problem or a failure, you get constricted. Thereby the solution to the problem is obstructed and you get disappointed. *When you realize that you don't have to look for the solution, then you have found the true solution. Just allow the solution to emerge.*

The mind tends to strengthen a problem by resisting it. Seeing the situation as a failure is the only failure. When you look at situations through the lens of your beliefs, you build resistance. Resistance causes the failure to persist.

It is important to remember that failures that occur at a given level of awareness can never be overcome at the same level of awareness. We need to raise our awareness to be able to witness clearly. With pure witnessing from a higher awareness, the failure no longer remains a failure. You begin to witness the beliefs and notions that are distorting your view, causing you to see it as a failure.

By being in the state of awareness, you allow the situation to settle in the space of acceptance. You no longer resist it. You don't get into a discord. You remain in harmony with the flow of whatever is happening. You remain aware of whatever is, without getting attached to it.

When you lend your detached presence through this way of witnessing, the solution emerges from the so-called failure itself. If the solution demands action, you will then witness all the necessary actions happening through you or whoever else participates in the scene.

You need to experience how solutions unfold from failures or setbacks when you abide as the witnessing presence. This will also build your conviction regarding your nature as pure *being*.

Every failure arrives with a gift

A failure comes with the sole purpose of giving you a gift. Albeit, in our ignorance, we continue to get distressed all our life over problems and failures. If we had the knowledge of solving problems, then we would be able to see the gift inside the problem. Simply by thinking about many things and seeing many incidents, we become overwhelmed and unhappy. We feel miserable if we have failed an exam, failed to get a promotion, lost a job, and so forth. If we look back and analyze the events of our past, we will realize that the incidents that we thought were a failure, have each given us a gift. We will realize how beautifully everything was happening; and we were getting anxious for no reason.

Therefore you have to attempt to search for the gift in every failure since every failure has not only the solution within it but also a gift. Those, in whose life no problems or failures arrive, remain dull and stupid throughout their life. Only those who face problems move ahead in life.

Only those plants that face many storms grow into strong trees. Those plants that never had to deal with any storm grow up to become trees that get uprooted by the first storm they face. While those that encountered and endured many a storm (problems) become strong to such an extent that later, however strong the winds blow, it makes no difference to them. Hence it has been said, "With every problem or failure arrives a gift."

Whenever a failure arrives, two points should be kept in mind. First, "What is the solution present in the failure?" Second, "What is the gift in it for me?" The gift is always present in the failure. You just need to attain the eye to see it. That eye, that perspective, is being

given to you through this knowledge. The perspective of seeing the truth is being given to you. Once you begin to see it, then it will be very easy to dissolve problems.

In the process of dissolving the problem, you will also receive an enormous gift. The more you see this gift, the more your happiness will continue to grow. Till date you may have received many gifts on your birthdays, anniversaries, festivals, parties, etc. When you open those gifts, how happy you feel! But this happiness decreases with time. On the other hand, if you go to the origin of the problem you are facing, you will get such a gift there, on opening which every time your joy goes on increasing. Your happiness will keep growing every day. You can receive such a gift. This gift is present behind your thoughts. Behind your thoughts, or in other words, behind your mind is your true essence, your real self. When you reach there through meditation, you will discover that you are not a limited individual. You are infinite and formless. All the problems that belong to the limited individual will dissolve.

Every failure is a ladder to success

There is a ladder in every failure. This can be compared to a springboard used to take a dive into the water. Depending on how big is the dive to be made, accordingly the diving board is placed. The bigger the leap, the higher is the springboard placed. The springboard is thus made according to the person who is going to take the dive. Just like the springboard, every failure is a ladder that you can use as a medium to take a leap into success. If you are able to make your failure the right medium, then you will climb the ladder of success and express the divine qualities lying dormant within you. The peak of Self Expression (expression of your true divine self) is scaled only through problems. Hence consider every problem and failure to be an opportunity to express Godly qualities and thereby derive happiness from them.

When you think about it, you will realize that you sit down to contemplate only due to those incidents that do not take place in your daily life but occur only once in a while. Otherwise, in our daily routine life we never contemplate. Our entire life is spent just like the bull which is tied to a pole and walks round and round. This bull is worked to extract oil from groundnut seeds. To prevent the bull from feeling giddy, its eyes are covered on the outer sides so that it cannot see on either side. It can only see forward. Thereby it's under the impression that it is going somewhere and hence keeps on walking, but in fact it is getting nowhere. It is just moving in a circle all the time. Our life also goes by in this manner, going around in circles of our daily routine; hence usually referred to as the 'daily grind'. Failures arrive to awaken us. Making them a stepping stone or a springboard, you should progress ahead. In order to cross a marshy patch, you drop a stone in it and use it as a stepping stone to cross the patch and move ahead. Similarly, the failure too is a stepping stone; you can step on it and get out of the marshy patch of your life.

You have come to Earth with a great purpose. Be careful lest you forget this purpose in worthless pursuits. When the question arises, "Why is this failure obstructing me?", then consider that failure to be a medium for your growth. Your journey should not stop because of that failure. It would indeed be a great loss if even after receiving such a precious opportunity of being born as a human, you get stuck midway in the journey without making use of this opportunity.

Once you have understood the true significance of failures arriving in your life, then later whenever a failure appears in your life, you will be thanking it. You will say, "It's good that this happened! If that failure had not cropped up, I would never have moved ahead. I was about to stop praying, thinking, contemplating, listening to the Truth, walking the path of Truth and helping others." Hence you should always be alert that whenever something troubles you, then without being troubled by it, you should make it a ladder. We need to understand that this failure is very essential to keep us awake. Otherwise we would go into sleep, live unconsciously, and continue to consider only ourselves to be knowledgeable. We will then be unable to dissolve our problems and instead drown in them.

While living in this world we face many kinds of problems and failures. Unmarried people face different failures; married people face different failures; those who have children face different failures; those who do not have children face different failures. Everybody encounters different failures. Everybody has different questions. The failures of some are related to children, job, or business. Whereas the failures of some others are related to mental issues such as fear, stress, worry, anger, etc. What we need to understand with all these issues is that failures have to be made a medium for our growth. When you stop in the path of progress, then life introduces some failures to awaken you. Otherwise man does not want to move ahead. Until you achieve complete development, you should not take anything that obstructs you as a failure, but as a stepping stone or a spring board. By stepping on this failure, you can take a leap to reach the peak of development.

The world is a game of snakes and ladders, and spirituality is the knowledge to convert snakes into ladders. To convert snakes into ladders implies how to make use of a "negative event" like failure. The snakes in our life are failures, problems, or setbacks that prevent us from attaining true happiness. These can be converted into ladders to attain happiness and success.

Some people get depressed about failure and on top of that they feel unhappy about that depression as well. They keep thinking, "Why am I so depressed?" But they should be told, "Congratulations." Why? Because it is a fact that those who get depressed are the ones who become Truth seekers. You will come to know that depression makes you move forward in life, because you try to find out: What is the ultimate truth? Why do we suffer? What is the reason? Can we change our thoughts? Is there something permanent and steady within us? Where should we search for it? With what perspective should we look at life, at our successes and failures? Questions like these can start your quest for the Truth.

So don't get scared when depression sets in. You are stressed out and you worry about *why* you are stressed. This is stress upon stress. Avoid this. Some people when they feel angry get more furious thinking *why* they became angry. It is okay to be angry, but anger upon your anger is harmful. If you just understand that we don't have to get angry upon our anger or depressed upon our depression, it will be great. If stress or depression has set in, just see what will it do, where will it take you. It has definitely come to make you do something that is essential for your growth. Later in life you will say, "It's good that I got stressed/depressed. It is due to it that I have progressed and attained success and happiness." Those who never get distressed, never achieve anything great in life. They always remain mediocre.

Every failure brings a lesson

A failure is not a trouble-maker, but a tuition teacher. In every failure there lies a hidden lesson.

If someone faces a financial failure, due to which he learns to save money, then this habit of saving can forever free him from financial problems. A person facing a money-related problem asked himself, "What is the lesson for me in this problem?" He then learnt financial planning and proper investment. He also developed respect for money, the habit of saving, and the habit of not spending on worthless pursuits.

If somebody has failing health due to an illness, he can learn from this illness too. If such a person learns the importance of regular physical exercise, then he will enjoy good health for the remainder of his life.

Someone fails at work due to inability to complete his tasks and projects on time. From this failure, if he learns how to manage and plan his time (time management), then his work will begin to get completed well before time and he will enjoy success throughout his life.

Some face failures in their relationships. They are always victims of misunderstandings. People are unable to understand them. Due to this problem, if they learn the importance of communication and the art of expressing themselves clearly, then this lesson will provide them the joy of pleasant relationships. In the problem of relationships is hidden the lesson of human psychology and human relations. This lesson will help them a lot in living together with everyone around lovingly and happily.

A student fails in his tests due to always postponing his studies till the eleventh hour. From this failure, if he learns the lesson of getting rid of procrastination and developing the habit of studying regularly, then he will be able to face all his upcoming tests without any stress and achieve success.

If a person has faced some failure and developed the problem of often sinking into depression, then from this attack of depression he can learn the lesson of: How to meditate? How to realize one's true self? How to surrender oneself in divine devotion, how to surrender stress, problems, and worries to the Almighty? Due to this lesson he will live his entire life filled with the bliss of divine devotion.

What is your lesson in the failure you have faced? And have you learned the lesson? This lesson will help you achieve success in your endeavor.

Failures are a challenge

When you play a game, you don't say, "Why should I stand in this very position? Why should I stay between these two lines? Why can't I run outside these lines? Why is there a limitation in this game?" This is because you know that you have been given these boundary lines in order to make the game interesting and exciting.

A question may arise in one's mind, "If we are the formless and infinite Self, then why are we attached to a single body? Why can't we go outside it?" The answer to this question too is that this boundary of the body (this limitation) is a rule of the game on Earth, which is a challenge for you. The purpose of this challenge is to derive maximum joy from this game of life. In spite of this challenge, if you want to know the secrets underlying this universe and you are able to know them, then it can be said that you have become an expert in this game. In spite of many limitations such as the lack of money, pains of the body, taunts of people, lack of strength, lack of time, spending a lot of time to earn your livelihood, and so on, if you are still able to express your true self, then you will be called a successful player. In order to become a successful player in the game of life, learn to accept the challenge of your limitations.

In the board game of carrom, you accept the rule of staying between two lines. By using the striker placed between the two limiting lines, you need to pocket the carrom coins. In the same way, even though the real you is formless and infinite, you need to accept the challenge of being within this limited body and becoming an expert at this game being played on Earth. This game will sometimes bring you success and sometimes failure. When you begin, you will find it very troublesome. You may feel, "I'm not able to do this; it's not possible." But gradually as you keep trying through regular practice, you will see that every failure is a challenge and it is becoming a ladder for your success.

In this world there are many people who are deaf, dumb, blind or handicapped in other ways, and are facing a lot of difficulties. You may be aware that in video games, as you reach the higher levels, the game becomes more challenging. But if you have become an expert, then you willingly and happily take on those challenges and play at the higher levels. Similarly, people with handicaps are higher players. They have chosen to play this Earthly game with these extra challenges and are playing at a higher level. If they are reminded of this truth, they can happily take on their challenges and overcome failures. There have been numerous examples of handicapped people who have attained tremendous success.

On the other hand, those who do not have any handicaps should realize that this is a great responsibility upon them. If they are free from all problems, then they should become instrumental in liberating others from their problems. This understanding is important for them that now their responsibility has increased. If you do not have problems in your life, then become responsible and help others to come out of their problems. Express your gratitude to God for not having any problems and accept a new challenge.

When you are able to see every failure as an opportunity, and realizing your responsibility you accept the challenge and become instrumental in helping others, if you learn your lesson, climb the ladder, reach the pinnacle of growth, if you are able to find the solution to a failure as well as extract its gift, then you will not find any failure to be a failure at all. Then your only failure, i.e. considering an incident to be a failure, will vanish.

SUMMARY:

1. Seeing a situation as a failure is the only failure.
2. The solution to a problem lies within the problem itself. In most cases, the solution appears as soon as the problem is correctly understood.

3. With pure witnessing from a higher awareness, the solution emerges from the so-called failure itself.

4. If we look back and analyze the events of our past, we will realize that the incidents that we thought were a failure, have each given us a gift.

5. Those, in whose life no problems or failures arrive, remain dull and stupid throughout their life. Only those plants that face many storms grow into strong trees.

6. In every failure there lies a hidden lesson, which when learnt can propel us towards success.

7. Life on Earth is a challenging game. Through regular practice in this game, you will find that every failure is a challenge and it is becoming a ladder for your success.

8. When you stop in the path of progress, life introduces some failures to awaken you. Otherwise you would go into sleep and live unconsciously.

9. The peak of Self Expression (expression of your true divine self) is scaled only through problems. Hence consider every problem and failure to be an opportunity to express Godly qualities and thereby derive happiness from them.

10. Once you have understood the true significance of failures arriving in your life, then later whenever a failure appears in your life, you will be thanking it.

* * *

Luminous Lives

WALT DISNEY

> *"All our dreams can come true,
> if we have the courage to pursue them."*
> — Walt Disney

The life of Walt Disney is a very interesting and inspiring one. Disney transformed the entertainment industry into what we know today. He created a world of magic, whimsy, and optimism. He pioneered the field of animation and found new ways to teach, educate, and have fun like children. He is the creator of one of the world's largest and most famous theme parks— Disneyland. "It's kind of fun to do the impossible." This shows the personality and attitude of this man who had the courage to fulfil his dreams.

Busy Childhood

On examining the life of Walt Disney, we can see various failures that preempted his successes. Walt Disney was born on December 5, 1901 in Chicago. His father Elias was a farmer and a businessman with little success. Walt spent some part of his childhood in a farm, where he developed a love of animals and an interest in drawing. When he was 10 years old, his family moved to Kansas City. Walt and his brother Roy woke up at 3:30 every morning to deliver newspapers before school as well as after school. The schedule was exhausting, and Walt often received poor grades due to falling asleep in class, but he continued his paper route every day—be it rain or shine—for more than six years. According to some biographical accounts, his father was a stern man who could have a strong temper at times, and would take the money his sons earned for "safekeeping", considering them too young to know the value of money. If his children misbehaved, he would not hesitate in punishing them with a cane. During this time, Walt also attended Saturday courses at the Kansas City Art Institute and took a correspondence course in cartooning.

Walt later worked in his father's jelly factory, then as a night guard, and then as a substitute deliveryman for the post office. At the age of 16, Disney attempted to enlist for the United States Army to fight against the Germans in World War I, but was rejected for being too young. He joined the Red Cross and was shipped to France, where he worked for a year as an ambulance driver.

Early career

After returning from France, he applied for a job as a cartoonist in a newspaper, but was rejected. He did not give up and found a job at a small art studio, but was laid off within a short time. He then found a job at Kansas City Film Ad Company, where along with Ub Iwerks, he started working on animated advertisements for local businesses. He was an untiring and courageous worker, who was not afraid at the prospect of doing thousands of drawings. At the age of 20, he experimented with many animation forms with a rented camera in his brothers' garage, where he produced short cartoons called laugh-o-grams. These were successful, which led to the establishment of Laugh-O-Gram Studio, but lack of funds soon began to take its toll. The company was down to its last penny, when a dentist asked Walt to make a promotional dental video. Walt did not even have money for repairing his shoes. The dentist paid him for his shoe repair as well as money for the video.

This could not save Walt's studio from closing down, but succeeded in recharging his ambition.

Moving to Hollywood

Walt decided to make a new beginning in Hollywood. He would hang around movie studios, watching and learning. He distributed copies of his animated film *Alice's Wonderland* and managed to get a contract from a distributor for a series of six films. This led him to build the *Disney Brothers Studio* in association with his brother. The studio had a roller coaster journey. At one point, he lost all his staff as well as the rights to a successful animated character he had created. He had to begin anew and that is when he created the legendary character Mickey Mouse. However, the costs were mounting and his studio was in debt. He had a fall-out with his distributor, which resulted in a nervous breakdown. He recovered from it with the help of his wife, changed his distributor, and then rose to the pinnacle of success.

In 1932, the first color cartoon *Flowers and Trees* won Walt the first of his studio's Academy Awards. In 1937, he released *The Old Mill*, the first short subject to utilize the multi-plane camera technique, which won him another Oscar. Walt Disney had now become a well-known name all over the country. *Snow White*, the first full-length animated musical feature, premiered in December 1937 to high praise from critics and audiences. It went on to become the most successful sound film made to that date. This brought a huge change in the company's fortunes and Walt's creativity. He believed, "All our dreams can come true, if we have the courage to pursue them."

Disneyland

After many more ups and downs in his production of numerous animated as well as live-action movies, Disney turned to his other dream. He wanted to build a clean and organized amusement park where children and their parents could have fun. It was no easy feat. Extensive research, planning, and designing was done but there were difficulties in obtaining funding. However, Walt was so keen to fulfill his dream that he had to investigate new methods of fundraising. He created a new show *Disneyland* for a fledgling TV company 'ABC' in return for which the network agreed to help finance the park. That show was very successful, which led to Disney's first daily television program, *The Mickey Mouse Club,* a variety show catering specifically to children. The program was accompanied by merchandising through various companies. After this, everything changed for ABC, Walt Disney Company, and Americans. Walt Disney's television show became the world's most favorite program and Disney acquired land about 50 miles south of Hollywood at Anaheim. It is here that Disneyland was opened to people for the first time in July 1955. After some initial hitches, it became a hit. Every year, millions of people from around the world visit Disneyland and various other Disney Parks. America started to be known for Disneyland. As he rightly put it: "If you can dream it, you can do it."

Honors and Awards

Despite all the hurdles and setbacks, Disney made his mark in the world. He won 22 Oscars, which are the most Academy Awards ever earned by an individual. He was given the Presidential Medal of Freedom in 1964, one of America's two highest civilian honors, and received more than 950 honors and citations throughout the world. While he passed away in 1966, he lives on through his ever-popular cartoons, movies, and magical parks. His recipe for success was the four Cs: Curiosity, Confidence, Courage, and Constancy. He said that "the greatest of these is confidence. Without confidence, you won't get past the challenges and critics that stand before you." He is the epitome of keeping your morale high when failure stares in your face. In his inimitable style he said, "You may not realize it when it happens, but a kick in the teeth may be the best thing in the world for you." This is what he had learnt from all the setbacks that he had encountered and overcome in his life.

∙ ∙ ∙

Spiritual Secret 4

THE WORLD IS AN ARRANGEMENT

*The world is a beautiful arrangement for you
to experience the impact of your thoughts and beliefs.*

Your thoughts have tremendous power. You attract everything in your life according to the thoughts you think. Your thoughts are like orders that you place to the universe, and the universe fulfills them accordingly. If you think positively, you attract positive events and people in your life. If you think negatively, you attract negative events and people. Hence it is generally believed that failures arise from negative thoughts. While that's true, you may be surprised to learn that some of the events you view as negative are actually the results of your higher orders—your positive thoughts.

For example, if you deeply wish for your career to be successful in a short time, you may very well be confronted with a series of challenges in order for this to happen. If you do not know this, you would probably view these growing pains and the stress related to them as negative. In reality, they have appeared because of your prayers—your higher orders. In this case, they are part of your orders for a rapidly successful career. There are skills, knowledge, and experiences you must have, and you must change the way you view things before you succeed in your career. Challenging situations appear in your life in order to impart you with higher qualities and virtues.

In this way, everything, every failure, setback, frustration, challenge, obstacle, or struggle becomes a powerful teacher, a mysterious gift, and an elevating springboard! This understanding in itself will help you access the divine self within and entertain only happy thoughts even in the midst of struggles.

It immensely helps to be constantly aware that your life situations resonate with the choices you make. Every failure, every situation in life that seems to be painful or frustrating, has been consciously or unconsciously chosen by you in your past, so as to enable you to mature and learn vital lessons—lessons of tenacity, patience, perseverance, compassion, and being in harmony with life itself.

No incident or situation is a failure by itself. A situation is a situation—as is. It becomes a so-called failure or triggers blame or complaint within us only because we are viewing it through the filters of our limiting beliefs.

You may have heard that the world is your mirror. But what does it mean? It means that your world appears to you as per the beliefs you hold. If you believe life is hard, or it's difficult to earn money or be successful, or people are deceitful—then that's exactly what you will find in the world. You may have seen people who don't have such beliefs, and hence life and people are good for them. This happens because of the universal principle: *You receive evidence for whatever you choose to believe.* And when you get the evidence, your belief becomes even more strong, and eventually it becomes your indisputable truth.

How does *your* world resonate with you?

Let us consider some more examples to understand how your world resonates with you.

If people are not helping you, it means that hidden inside you is the belief that people are not helpful. This gets reflected as evidences in your world. It could also mean that somewhere you are not helping yourself. If people are rude to you, it does not necessarily mean that you are rude to others, but it may mean that your belief that others are rude is causing incidents where people are rude to you repeatedly.

If you have anger within you, you will see and hold others as the reason for making you angry. You will also tend to see more anger in others, and believe that they are unnecessarily angry towards you when it's not your fault. The truth is that you are angry with yourself, so you view others as being angry or as the cause of your anger.

If one keeps complaining that other people are not committed, it could possibly mean that somewhere the person is not committed to oneself. Since a lack of commitment is an issue from within, the person projects and complains that most people aren't committed. There are leaders who command respect, love, and commitment from people. This is because these leaders are committed to themselves. They do not lack commitment. As a result, they do not see a lack of commitment in others; and automatically people are committed to them.

The following scenario occurs every day in classrooms. Students are calm and orderly for one teacher, yet they bring the roof down during another teacher's class. The key is not inherent in the thinking of the students, but in how the teacher thinks and deals with herself. The first teacher listens to herself. Automatically, as the world is a mirror, others listen to her. The second teacher is likely to be someone who does not believe in herself. So, automatically, others do not take her seriously.

Thus, your world is a screen upon which you project your own mental traits, your unresolved emotions, your strengths and deficiencies. What you view as the world is, in reality, a reflection of what you project.

Have you ever wondered why different people react to the same events in sometimes vastly different ways?

That's because they are projecting or superimposing their own mental baggage onto the screen, then watching the scene through their own mental filters. When they do this, it distorts the picture of reality.

There is no absolute world *out there*. Rather, you are constantly shaping your own personalized world as you go through life. People, situations, the weather—everything you experience—are shaded by your perception and are projections of what is held deep within your mind.

You mold the personalities of people around you through your own beliefs and assumptions. This occurs without your awareness, and you may probably find yourself criticizing people for shortcomings that are merely a projection of your own beliefs. You experience your own unresolved emotions by unknowingly projecting them on people. So, when someone seems to be angry or deceitful to you, he or she is actually reflecting the anger or deceit which is unresolved within you!

What happens in the outside world is a reflection—a resonance—of what is happening within you. Everything around you resonates with what's going on within your mind.

This may seem a bit farfetched to believe in the beginning, but when you experiment with this secret, you will see how this secret has been functioning infallibly. Though it may seem unbelievable, you're actually attracting situations and people into your daily life according to the mental traits (positive and negative), emotions, and deficiencies you harbor within your mind. You are lost in external details to such an extent that you don't realize these details are only living pictures of what lies buried within your mind.

External situations are not the cause, but rather a reflection of what you hold within.

Suppose it is raining and you hate it. Rain is simply water falling from the sky. However, your reality is more than just information; it is your experience shaded by your perception. Your perception of the information creates your experience or your reality. The experience of your world is the result of your perception and interaction with information. You may sulk and complain about a rainy day but do you ever consider why you believe a rainy day to be worthy of a bad mood? Or is it based on some past impression or conditioning? "These rains are so irritating. They have washed out my plans!" is your *perception* and *interpretation.*

If rain makes you angry, it could be because of your past impressions: perhaps it ruined a special day at the park, or you remember the time your basement was flooded. It could even be from past conditioning—maybe your parents always disliked the rain because the children came home with muddy shoes.

Try comparing your negative interpretation of rain to a farmer's. A farmer may love the rains and feel ecstatic since his crops are being watered! It's a matter of perception and context.

So, is one of you wrong and the other right? Of course not. Each person's reality is 100% real, true, and valid to them and it depends on their individual context and conditioning.

If one person at a party feels that it's a fun group of people, full of stimulating conversation, and another person finds the party boring, it's a matter of perception. It's the same party, same people, but two different experiences!

How to Look at the World?

You can utilize the way the world appears to you as a mirror to think deeply about the inner workings of your own mind. It is meant for you to look within yourself, to learn more about how you are actually creating your own life situations, including failures, through the way you think.

If you can develop this understanding and become aware of the projection that is constantly occurring in your daily life situations, you can actually use these situations to recognize the distortions that are present within your mind. You can then be open to the possibility of clearing such distortions that may exist in your perspective.

For example, if you are engrossed in some urgent or important work, you do not pay much attention to people around you. That does not mean that you do not like them. But if someone else does the same to you, you may misinterpret their actions and create a story in your mind that they are ignoring you and they don't like you. This fallacy takes root in your mind and could be the cause of unhappiness within you.

In ignorance, people create such stories from childhood, and sometimes carry them throughout their lives. These stories vary according to their environment and their upbringing. These stories can be related to joy, sorrow, success, failure, self-image, self-belief, and other aspects of life. They live their entire lives based upon these make-believe stories.

These stories are the foundation of your thought framework. Often, at the root, there are just a few stories. They are the base on which the rest of your thinking, conclusions, actions, and even experiences are based.

Imagine the power that the breaking of even one such story can bring. It can pierce an entire family of thoughts and perceptions based on it, which were unknown to you. The results can be so dramatic that in many cases you won't even know how you became free from the grip of certain vices or habits that had bound you.

Introspection can reveal these underlying stories that the mind has held deeply since childhood. The moment these stories are clearly brought to light, they are automatically replaced by a clearer undistorted view of the world. This way, you can raise yourself beyond the limitations of your past conditioning.

If you are not aware of this secret, you can easily pass judgment about an incident, or a person, without knowing the reality. By truly understanding this secret, you can give up this habit of judging and taking your interpretation of an event as the undisputed truth. If you were considering an event to be your "failure", your perception will undergo a radical change. In fact, you will be amazed by the fact that all the events that were the cause of your suffering have become the cause of your joy.

Change Your World

If you don't like the "reality" of your life, the fascinating thing is that *you can change it*. You can release yourself from your perspective by being aware that your reality is only *a* reality, not *the only* reality. See your reality as one possible way of perceiving things.

When you drop your preconceived perspectives and access the Self within, you become open to this. If you are not aware of your perspective, it can dictate your attitude and your experience.

The power of loving acceptance is the key to transcend the limiting beliefs about joy, sorrow, success, failure, that resonate as your world. To release the beliefs that you have held within, you need to first bring them to light and accept them completely. Heal all such deep-seated impressions through the practice of forgiveness. First forgive yourself and then ask for forgiveness from the Self for having held those impressions. Also ask for forgiveness from the Self for all those who were responsible for the creation of those impressions, including yourself. Love the part of the world that appears faulty and it will start healing.

This secret also teaches us that we should not focus on the faults of others. Instead, we should look within. To attain our highest potential, we must first get rid of our flaws. We must begin by refusing to focus on the faults of others. *The real fault lies in the blaming eye that sees faults in the world.* Our focus on those faults—meaning the fact that we notice them in the external world—is a reflection of a part of our own inner world. This gives us the opportunity to improve ourselves.

When resistance to something builds within you, when you have constant complaints about something, you become like an element that attracts negativities. You want to be a magnet that attracts the highest possibilities into your life. Instead of complaining, give your attention to what you want to see.

When you truly comprehend the world as a mirror, then this understanding enables you to give your attention precisely to what you want to create in your life, instead of focusing on the faults of others.

Whatever you see in the world is telling you the truth about yourself. Otherwise, how will you know yourself? *The eye needs a mirror to see itself.* Similarly, a person needs a mirror in the form of relationships and incidents to recognize the faults within.

We need to ask ourselves honestly: Am I prepared to be free from all the false beliefs that have accumulated over this lifetime? Am I ready to let go of my old beliefs about success and failure? If the answer is yes, then we need to give up our complaints and look within.

Discover how and in which relationships you have been creating suffering for yourself and others. Inquire into your own thoughts honestly, in a new manner. Use every complaint to look within and achieve clarity. Instead of working on changing others, we need to work on changing ourselves.

There is only one person who is capable of setting limits to your growth. It is YOU.

You are the only person who can transform your life. You alone can influence your happiness and your success. You are the only one who can help yourself.

Your life does not change when your boss changes, or when your friends change. Your life is not waiting for your parents or partner to change. Your life changes when YOU change. When you go beyond your limiting beliefs and realize that you are the only one responsible for your life.

The most important relationship you can have is the one you have with yourself. Examine yourself. Don't be afraid of difficulties or losses. Be a winner; shape your reality by shaping yourself.

Once you focus inward and work on overcoming your shortcomings, the world will not appear the same. Gradually, you will begin to realize that this world is a marvelous system that resonates with your nature. It will begin to look more beautiful to you. You will be able to forgive people without complaining about them.

The day you find everyone beautiful and start liking everyone will be the day you have become a beautiful and successful person in the true sense. You will have learned to see the Self or the Source functioning through every human being. And then the world around you will change!

SUMMARY:

1. It is generally believed that failures arise from negative thoughts.

While that's true, some of the events you view as negative are actually the results of your higher orders.

2. Every failure, every situation in life that seems to be painful or frustrating, has been consciously or unconsciously chosen by you in your past, so as to enable you to mature and learn vital lessons.

3. A situation is a situation—as is. It becomes a so-called failure or triggers blame or complaint within us only because we are viewing it through the filters of our limiting beliefs.

4. Your world appears to you as per the beliefs you hold. You receive evidence for whatever you choose to believe.

5. Your world is a screen upon which you project your own mental traits, your unresolved emotions, your strengths and deficiencies. What you view as the world is, in reality, a reflection of what you project.

6. What happens in the outside world is a reflection—a resonance—of what is happening within you. Everything around you resonates with what's going on within your mind.

7. The world is our mirror. If we can see faults in others, it means that those faults lie within us. To attain our highest potential, we must first get rid of our faults.

8. There is only one person who is capable of setting limits to your growth. It is YOU.

9. Your life is not waiting for others to change. Your life changes when YOU change.

10. The day you find everyone beautiful and start liking everyone will be the day you have become a beautiful and successful person in the true sense.

**

> "I am grateful for all of my problems.
> After each one was overcome, I became stronger
> and more able to meet those that were still to come.
> I grew in all my difficulties."
> — J. C. Penney

VOICE OF FAITH
TO SHIFT FROM FAILURE TO SUCCESS

I have clear understanding and I am ready to change with time.

I easily and happily let go of the old and welcome the new.

I am the operator of my brain and mind.

It is easy to mold my mind to a new thought pattern.

I am free of my old mindset.

I am releasing my old thinking that hinders my progress.

I am ready for supreme success.

Spiritual Secret 5

HIGHEST CHOICES LEAD TO HIGHEST SUCCESS

Making the highest choice in every matter, big or small, results in a supreme life.

Each spiritual secret you encounter in this book builds on the previous one. So far we have seen how to accept failure and look at failure in a totally different light. Let us now understand what choices one should make on facing failure.

Each and every choice that we make in life impacts us. Hence we need to learn the art of consistently making the highest choice every moment in our life. This art will prove to be a blessing in the future.

The choices that we make in the present determine our future. That is why we need to ask ourselves, "What are the choices that I am making today? How is my future shaping up?" This applies to every minor as well as major choice. If we are facing a failure or a setback, the first question we need to ask is: "What is the highest choice I can make in this situation?" This question will save you from spiraling into negativity, which leads to regretful actions, like giving up or causing harm to oneself or others. These are lower choices. Additionally, this question will help you to shift from a negative mindset to a positive one. Hence you will be able to take steps in the right direction towards success and joy. This is because in a positive frame of mind, you will be able to accept the failure, and identify how "This is that what I need," or what is the gift, ladder, lesson, or challenge it has brought for you. Thus, after asking this powerful question of what is the highest choice in the given situation, you will be able to choose how you are going to gain from the failure instead of letting it pull you down. So, it all depends on the choice you make about how you are going to face failure. This will decide your future.

Being unaware that their choices are shaping their future, people continue to make choices in their everyday life without any thinking or contemplation. As a result, when they stumble upon an undesirable future created by their own choices, they cry out, "We never anticipated such a future!" We should clearly recognize that our future is the result of our own choices.

What is the highest choice?

A highest choice is one that is aligned with the purpose of your life. To be able to make the highest choice consistently, you need to make up your mind about what you wish to create in life. What is it that you are actually aspiring for, in and through all your pursuits? Once you have made up your mind, you can then constantly observe yourself and ask at every juncture, "Am I making the highest choice in accordance with my life purpose?"

When we are not clear about our life purpose, we tend to deviate in many different directions by entertaining aspirations that contradict one another. As a result, we ordain a mixed future of contradictions, which confuses us even further. For example, an engineer dreams of working on research projects in the labs of NASA. At the same time, if he does not wish to leave his home town to fulfill this dream, then these are mutually contradictory aspirations. As a result, he would waste a significant period of time making inappropriate choices. The result will be a confusing future which will be filled with dilemmas. Therefore it is essential to have clarity about your purpose of life and to carefully work out the smaller aims that can lead to the attainment of your life purpose.

If a student, who is supposed to study during a given period, instead wastes time in chatting, video games, or watching television, then he has not made the highest choice. These activities also lend shape to his future. If he fails in his exams, or does not score well, he may well complain, "I never desired this result. I wanted to pass the tests with good scores, but I cannot understand how I failed." He should instead ask himself what is the highest choice he can make now. The answer will arise that he should now focus on his studies.

Most people are not vigilant about the subtle choices that they make in their daily life. As a result, they do not recognize how they are shaping an undesirable future through their choices. In many cases, one may actually feel happy for the given moment in making a particular choice, but it is possible that it leads to an unfavorable future. The need is to raise the level of awareness and remain vigilant when a choice is to be made. If we are able to do so successfully, then we can consciously shape our future as we desire.

The art of making the highest choice

The art of making the highest choice can be acquired by asking the right question. Whatever situation we find ourselves in, or whatever activity we are engaged in, we should always question ourselves, "What is the highest choice that I can make at this moment?"

If an executive who works in an office fails at his job, his mind may bring up numerous excuses. The mind fools itself with justifications. Choosing to dwell on excuses and avoiding what needs to be done in the present will result in an undesirable future. Hence he should ask himself, "What is the highest choice I can make in this situation?"

Thus, we need to be alert about the choice that we are making at every juncture. We have to identify: When do we falter in our choices? When are our choices mediocre? And when do we make higher choices? To recognize this, it is helpful to practice self-observation. Relentlessly observe how you behave. Constantly assess the real drivers behind the decisions that you make. This has to be taken up without a break; there should be no time-off from self-observation.

If we are not alert about our choices we are making at present, then choices arise from our past programming or our preconditioning. The belief systems and behavioral patterns of people around us have a deep impact on our subconscious from our formative years. If we are not alert, then our preconditioning shapes our future; we then lead a mechanical life like robots.

When a person fails in a job interview and gets disappointed, he does not realize that he is actually choosing to be unhappy. Even the choice of being unhappy ordains a future. Choosing to be unhappy is certainly not a higher choice. But most people unconsciously continue to make this choice day after day. One who is vigilant about the choices that he makes will decide to remain happy despite such a failure. He will then be able to overcome the failure by accepting it and convert it into a blessing. Such a higher choice will yield a bright future. What would your choice be in such a situation?

An alcoholic or drug addict may choose to linger in the abyss of unconsciousness. Another addict may decide to visit a rehab center to overcome his addiction. Each one of them is choosing his future based on his level of awareness in the given situation. We can clearly see that the one who decides to undergo rehab is making the highest choice in the given situation. The other one who decides to remain steeped in intoxication is making a lower choice. He is choosing to create a hell for himself, while the other paves the way for a better future.

As with the minor, so with the major

Every time you decide something and then don't do it, it is akin to a mini-failure. Immediately become aware of the choice you can now make. If you don't feel like exercising although you had decided earlier, ask yourself immediately what is the highest choice possible in this situation.

If you choose to watch a game on TV when you are supposed to follow your daily exercise regimen, you end up skipping your exercises. After the game, you may choose to have breakfast, after which it will not be possible to exercise. In this way, the mind unconsciously postpones the exercise to the next day. However, if you choose to stick to your exercise regimen despite the distractions, then this is the highest choice.

You may wonder how a daily exercise regimen can be the "highest" choice? It seems to be such a trivial affair. How can the highest choice apply in such minor matters? This example illustrates that if we are able to make the right choices in minor or trivial matters, then our choices will naturally tend to be the highest in major or vital matters. If we are unable to make appropriate choices in trivial matters, then how can our key choices be right, for instance on facing a failure? As with the minor, so with the major. We need to be alert and ensure that we make the right choices regardless of whether the context is trivial or vital.

Easy options can be deceptive

True progress in life occurs when man exerts himself against the forces of his tendencies and pre-programmed behavioral patterns. However, given a chance, man tends to follow the path of least resistance and obeys the law of inertia. In order to avoid changing his predisposition, he flows with the tide of his tendencies by adopting shortcuts wherever possible.

Man falls to the temptations of sense gratification and of earning easy money; he rushes for quick fixes and gives lame excuses without realizing it. To earn fast bucks, he resorts to illegal and immoral practices. One cannot avoid the consequences of such shortcuts for long. Such a life that is based on lower choices of a weak character inevitably leads to the doldrums. Easy options may appear enticing on the surface. We may avoid exerting ourselves when thrown into situations by choosing easier options, but there is a high likelihood of losing our way by falling to such choices.

Whenever we are at a juncture where we need to take a major decision, we often find ourselves in a dilemma and feel tempted to choose easy options. We may decide to give up the endeavor or we may choose not to take any decision as we are afraid of the consequences. Choosing not to decide also brings its own future.

To avoid falling to the deception of easy options, we should be very clear about why we are choosing a given option. We need to ask ourselves the right questions:

1. Are our choices driven by the need to resist change and remain in our comfort zone?
2. Are we choosing impulsively in order to escape situations or challenges?
3. Are our choices driven by the genuine need for inner growth and developing our capabilities?

Your choice—a reflection of who you are

When we fail at something, then how do we respond? Our response is a reflection of who we are. The choices that we make in life serve as a reflection for us. It shows who we consider ourselves to be whilst making the choice. The inability to make decisions indicates weakness of character and lack of conviction about one's true nature. We need to ask ourselves, "Who am I considering myself to be when I am making this choice? Am I assuming myself to be a limited individual or the infinite and omnipotent Self?"

Making the highest choice may initially require some effort to overcome inertia and to set oneself free from the shackles of preconditioning. First, we need to at least try that 2 out of 10 choices that we make in a day are arising from higher awareness. The confidence that arises from being able to do so helps in increasing this to 4 out of 10, then to 8 out of 10. It will not be long before all our choices arise from the highest level of consciousness.

When you consistently make the highest choice, then life becomes a natural expression of gratitude and bliss. Soon you will find that higher choices begin to flow naturally from within. You will naturally keep away from lower or mediocre choices. Dilemmas of the past will give way to a sense of gratitude and clarity of purpose.

It helps to pause a bit before you ask yourself what is the highest choice. If you are facing a failure, dip into the Self through any meditation you can practice. Then ask yourself, what is the highest choice now? This will help you to make the choice without any conditioning of the past or fear of the future. It makes your choice conscious and increases your commitment towards the choice.

Thus, it is important to make the highest choice—be it regarding your goal, your decisions, or your thoughts, feelings, words, and actions. If you are serious and passionate about your goal, your choice will always be in the direction of your goal, even if a failure or setback has appeared. Before making any choice, you will be able to think whether this choice will lead to success or failure in achieving your goal. Thus, you will make the highest choice in every situation, so that you can attain your goal.

SUMMARY:

1. Each and every choice that we make in life impacts us. Hence, we need to learn the art of consistently making the highest choice.

2. Most people are not vigilant about the subtle choices that they are making in daily life. They do not recognize how they are shaping an undesirable future through their choices.

3. If we are facing a failure or a setback, the first question we need to ask is: "What is the highest choice I can make in this situation?"

4. If we are not alert about our choices, then these choices arise out of our past programming.

5. In order to be able to make the highest choice consistently, we need to be clear about what we wish to create in life. We need to diligently ask ourselves, "Am I making the highest choice in accordance with my life purpose?"

6. If we are unable to make appropriate choices in trivial matters, then how can our major choices be right?

7. To avoid falling to the deception of easy options, we should be very clear about why we are choosing a given option.

8. The choices that we make in life serve as a reflection for us. It shows who we consider ourselves to be whilst making the choice.

9. It helps to pause a bit, dip into the Self within, and then ask yourself what is the highest choice.

10. When we consistently make the highest choice, then life becomes a natural expression of gratitude and bliss.

* * *

Luminous Lives

MAHARSHI KARVE

Bestow your ears to listen to the supreme truth
Bestow your hands to serve others
Bestow your heart for divine devotion
And bequeath your ego to attain success.

Is it possible for failure to become the source of strength to attain success? Yes. The annals of history are replete with such examples, when upon encountering failure people became even more determined and resolved to achieve success. If we face failure with this knowledge, then success won't be far behind.

Let us look at the life of a great man who was a preeminent social reformer and who dedicated his life to empowerment of women—Maharshi Karve. Before Karve's time, Hindu social customs used to discourage education of girls, and parents routinely married off their daughters often before their puberty usually to young boys, but at times even to grown-up widowers. But remarriage of widows was disallowed, so if a breadwinning man died, his widow's remaining life would turn bleak because, lacking education, she could not support herself. She had to spend her life serving the household of her late husband's relatives. Moreover, widows were considered to be a curse and treated like outcasts in society.

Maharshi Karve was one of the pioneers in India in breaking with extraordinary fortitude and perseverance the above harsh social customs against womankind. He promoted education of women and freedom for widows to remarry. His journey was not an easy one, but he believed that where there is a will, a new path will surely emerge.

Once he said in a radio broadcast that he continues to discover many new paths and hence enjoys the bliss of life. His bliss was to provide education and reform the plight of women. He completely dedicated his life to this cause, sacrificed his own comfort and leisure, and also worked for the welfare of the *dalits* and the children of widows so that they could prosper too.

We often blame our fate and lament the lack of wealth, but Dr Karve was born to a lower middle-class family and completed his studies with money earned by providing private tutoring to children. He also established a university for women on his own steam, with just 5 students, which gradually developed into the SNDT University, which is now a symbol of excellence in higher education opportunities for women, and it includes 174 colleges all over India. The beginnings of this massive institution can be trailed to a dilapidated shanty in the remote village of Hingane.

Early life

Dhondo Keshav Karve was born on April 18, 1858, at Sheravali in Ratnagiri district, Maharashtra. His father was Keshav Karve who lived like a saint and his mother was a self-respecting woman. Karve was married at the age of 14 and his wife Radhabai was only 8 years old. Child marriage was prevalent in those times and the society had to suffer its negative consequences. Children were born weak and deficient, women would become old even before their prime age set in, and they also would be widowed at a very young age.

Karve was very interested in studies since childhood, but he had to face hurdles at every step. At the age of 18 he was still studying in Class

6 and had to appear for his examination in Mumbai or Satara, which were more than 100 miles away. He and some of his friends set out on foot through forests and mountains facing torrential rain to reach Satara. But to his utter disappointment, he was not allowed to appear for the examination because his physique defied his age. He was thin and short and did not appear to be 18 years old. He returned without taking the exam. But he did not give up. He appeared for the exam next year in Kolhapur and was successful.

Karve was inherently a social reformer. As a young boy, he would read out the newspaper for the villagers to listen and would also read their letters to them. His teacher Soman Guruji had instilled in him the importance of a high character and social welfare. This was the reason he could work well in the field of imparting education to widows.

Karve was keen on receiving modern education, which was not available in his village, and so his father sent him to Ratnagiri High school. But owing to health issues, he returned to his village. However, he was determined to study and so he went to Mumbai at the age of 20 to pursue his studies. He managed to earn the B.A. degree at the age of 27. One cannot imagine the joy of a student who completed his education after so many hurdles!

His life in Mumbai was simple but not without its share of problems. He had to meet his expenses by providing private tutoring to children and doing odd jobs. Despite working hard for every penny, he would always donate a certain portion of his earnings.

Career and Social Work

After completing his studies, Karve decided to take up a teaching career. However, during this time in 1891, his dear wife died at the age of 27, which was a devastating blow for him. Thereafter he began teaching in small schools, and after some time he got the job of teaching mathematics at the reputed Fergusson College in Pune. This paved the path for him to be a reformer because Pune was the intellectual capital of Maharashtra with a milieu of thinkers and reformers on one hand and fanatic traditionalists on the other.

Karve had been observing the deplorable condition of widows in the society and was deeply moved by it. Reformatory thoughts concerning the harsh social customs against womankind were stirring in his mind. Implementing his own reformatory thoughts with extraordinary courage, two years later, in 1893, he chose a widow as his second wife. This marriage created turmoil in the society. His family in the village was harassed and he was ostracized by his village due to which he could not meet his relatives or acquaintances. The more he was opposed, the more he became determined to work for the cause of women. He founded *Widhwa-Wiwahottejak Mandali* in the same year, which, besides encouraging marriages of widows, also helped the needy children of widows.

In 1896, when Karve started his shelter and school for widows, he had to start it in the remote village of Hingane outside the city of Pune because the dominant orthodox Brahmin community in the city had ostracized him for his reformatory activities. (Karve himself belonged to the Brahmin community.) Karve's 20-year-old widowed sister-in-law was the first to join his school. Due to his meager resources, for many years Karve would walk several miles from Hingane to Pune to teach mathematics at Fergusson College and also collect in his spare time paltry donations from a few progressive donors. People from the orthodox community would openly hurl insults at him when he went around to spread the word of his emancipatory work and collect donations. He would work in his shelter after finishing his college work and spend his own earnings on the shelter's operations. In 1914, he left his teaching job to fully dedicate his time to his cause.

After reading about Japan Women's University in Tokyo, Karve felt inspired to establish in 1916 in Pune the first university for women in India, with just five students. During 1917–1918, he established the Training College for Primary School Teachers and another school for girls. In 1920, an industrialist and philanthropist, Vithaldas Thackersey, gave a large donation to Karve's university, which was then renamed as SNDT Indian Women's University.

In 1929 and 1930, Karve toured various countries of the world and lectured at various forums on women's education and social reforms in India. In 1931, the SNDT University established its first college in Mumbai. In 1936, Karve started the Maharashtra Village Primary Education Society with the goal of opening primary schools in villages that had no schools run by the district local boards. He also encouraged maintenance of reading habits of adults in villages. In 1944, he founded the *Samatā Sangh* (Association for the Promotion of Human Equality). In 1949, the Government of India recognized SNDT University as a statutory university.

Karve had four children, all of whom rose to eminence in their own fields of work.

Besides dedicating his life to the emancipation of women in India, Karve stood for the abolition of the caste system and the curse of untouchability in Hindu society. In 1958, the Government of India awarded him its highest civilian award, the *Bharat Ratna*, and also issued stamps to commemorate his 100th birthday. After India's independence, it was the first time a living person was pictured on stamps.

Despite a humble background and countless adversities, Karve, along with other stalwarts, succeeded in bringing about a revolution in society with dedication, integrity, and resolve. He proved that where there is a will there is a way. If women and widows get more respect today, if the women of India today are no less than men in the field of education or career, it is all because of the selfless and dedicated service of people like Dr Karve. Hence Dr Karve is affectionately called by the people of India as *Annasaheb,* which means elder brother, and with deep respect and honor as *Maharshi Karve*—*Maharshi* meaning 'a great sage.'

• • •

Spiritual Secret 6

FEAR OF FAILURE STOPS YOUR PROGRESS

*Unless you stop trying, you have not failed.
Hence, never give up due to fear of failure.*

Fear of failure stops man from progressing. Actual failure is only when one stops trying. Hence, don't quit due to fear of failure. Fear, especially of what people might say, is a major obstacle in the way of achieving supreme success. If people can ridicule and criticize Einstein or Edison, they can ridicule and criticize you too. But their words can affect you, only if you allow them to. So, don't allow them. Keep trying to achieve what you want. Fearful thoughts prevent you from opening up and blossoming in life. Hence, let us take a look at some practical tools to transcend fears.

"In spite of"

It is normal to feel fearful when trying something once again after encountering failure or when starting with something new. Do not enforce a condition upon yourself that you shouldn't feel fear. This condition imposed by the mind is baseless. Let your mind not impose any conditions. To do so, remember the words "in spite of." In spite of feeling fear, go ahead and do whatever you *can* do.

Tell your mind, "Show me that you can do whatever is *possible* for you. In spite of feeling fear, can you take just one step forward?" Then go ahead and take the first step. Here are some examples of what to say to yourself using "in spite of":

- In spite of the fear of rejection, I will face this interview.
- In spite of the fear that my business idea might fail, I will attempt to garner the required investment.
- In spite of the fear that my relation may be spoilt, I will give honest feedback to my friend—gently.

Every individual who has achieved success in life has felt some amount of fear before taking up challenges. But they could achieve success because they went ahead in spite of fear. You too have to go ahead with whatever is possible for you, in spite of fear.

Don't keep languishing in apprehensions whether you will achieve success or not. You are programmed for success. If you keep your focus on abundance and success, you will definitely achieve them.

Face the fear

From time to time, we experience certain essential and certain unessential fears. These keep fluctuating according to situations. The best way to achieve freedom from fears is to face them. Make a list of the activities you are afraid of doing. Then start doing them one by one. For example, your fears may include speaking on stage, facing authority figures, trying again after failure or rejection, standing up for yourself, asking questions to teachers, speaking to strangers, playing with dogs, standing at heights, paying last respects to deceased people, etc. Experiment with directly facing your fears. The more you face the fear, the more you will become desensitized to the fear.

Other than facing your fears, also make a list of the things that have made you feel successful. By recalling such incidents and reliving the experience of success, your self-confidence will rise. This self-confidence will motivate you to perform tasks that were earlier difficult for you.

The two exercises above can work together to help you gain adequate courage, firm faith, and strong resolve.

Affirmations

Be aware of what you think or say, for the universe may manifest them into your reality. Hence always think positively and choose positive words.

Here are some suggested affirmations that you could repeat to yourself every night before sleep. These will help remove the fears hidden deep within your mind.

- I am courageous because I have stopped fearing fear. I have become friends with fear.
- I am God's property. No failure can touch me. My success is assured.
- Good and courageous people are entering my life.
- Every day, in every way, my body-mind is becoming better and better.
- I am God's student. I cannot fail in any examination.
- God's loving energy is always guiding me in the right direction.
- That which does not kill me makes me stronger.

By affirming these powerful statements repeatedly and with faith, your life will be filled with fearlessness and courage.

Remove ignorance about failure

Ignorance about failure creates fear about failure. People are not aware that failure is a stepping stone on the path of success and can even turn out to be a blessing. In most people, the ignorance about failure resides deep within the mind. Just before achieving success, the self-talk that goes on in their minds is: "Am I going to fail? Are the tables going to turn on me? How will I face people if I fail? What will I tell them?" Such thoughts pull them towards failure because thoughts—whether negative or positive—have the power to manifest into reality.

Failure can even lead people to commit suicide. Thoughts of failure and suicide often walk hand-in-hand. Everyone should be made to understand that if 'life' were placed on one side of a weighing scale and 'failure' on the other, then 'life' would turn out to be much heavier of the two. We have received life for a reason: to learn. Each one of us should repeat this thought to ourselves: "Moving ahead is safe for me and it is also the will of God."

Successful people never indulge in negative self-talk. Their thoughts always remain positive. As a result, they find a new direction even in failures. They have the understanding that failure is not unsafe; it is very much safe.

Never stop learning and performing new experiments on facing failure. In any experiment, whether it is a success or a failure, the important thing is learning. How will you learn if you stop experimenting due to fear of failure? Experiments are nothing but creative actions to tackle difficulties in life. Man shines after going through difficult challenges.

Create a new future with new thinking

If you think that you will continue to fail because of encountering only failures in the past, then it's time to break this illusion. Due to the experience of failure getting embedded in your mind, the fear of failure remains alive within you. Unknowingly this fear attracts failure again and again. Therefore you need to come out of this vicious cycle. You can do this by focusing on success instead of failure. Believe in success, think about success, talk about success, and feel success. This will pull success towards you.

There is one more important aspect to understand. Often one thinks that any activity that does not yield any profit is useless. But this is not so. Nothing you do goes to waste. Every activity you do, whether successful or not, provides you with 'experience'. Experience trains you. And training prepares you for highest success.

See failures as scientists do

When you fail at something, try and change your method of working. This is what scientists do. By doing an old job in a new way, a new discovery can occur. By trying out a variety of methods, it is possible to settle upon the best one.

Edison had to experiment with thousands of ways before he could find the one that produces light in a bulb. When asked whether he felt disappointed on failing so many times, he replied, "I have not failed. I've just found 10,000 ways that won't work." Edison had such a unique perspective on failure that he never felt the sadness of failure.

Failure is not how it appears to you. Failure is how *you think it to be*. If your perspective is right, failure is your teacher. Else, it is despair.

Dwell in the feeling of 'I have'

The feeling of 'I have' has so much power that it can overcome most of your fears. Many a time, our goal eludes us in spite of enormous efforts. Thereby a feeling of 'I don't have' begins to develop. This feeling halts the success that was headed your way. The feeling of 'I have', on the other hand, acts like a magnet.

A person was unable to find a job. He applied to several companies but did not get any interview calls. After a lot of efforts, he managed to find a small job. "Something is better than nothing," he said to himself and accepted the job. In a few days, miracles started happening. He started getting interview calls for good jobs. He passed several interviews and received several job offers.

The reason for this is when he got his first job, the feeling of 'I don't have' changed to 'I have.' His anxiety and worry were replaced by a positive feeling. This positive mindset started working like a magnet for better jobs.

A woman had failed to conceive despite several treatments. Finally, she and her husband adopted a child. After a brief period of time, this woman became pregnant! You may have heard of such miracles. This occurred because as soon as she adopted a child, her feeling of 'I don't have' changed to 'I have.'

Here is an experiment you can perform to understand this point. If you have a friend or an acquaintance who doesn't have a job, offer him or her a small task and pay them, even if it is a miniscule amount. Or arrange for them to join a part time job. This will help because their feeling of 'I don't have a job' will change to 'I have a job.' This will work like a magnet and attract the job they want.

You can try this experiment on yourself in case you are the one without a job. If you have a friend or acquaintance who runs a business, you can tell him or her, "Hey, let me help out for a month or two. You can worry about paying me later. Paying me a small amount based on the value I generate will also do. Let me try my hand at anything you need." Hopefully, your friend may accept the offer. The chances are that you will attract the right opportunity for you by the change in feeling that occurs once you start doing the temporary job in your friend's business. Try it out to experience miraculous results. Get to know how nature's laws work and become fearless.

Stop focusing on "what people will say"

Instead of focusing on "what people will say," focus on "what's the right thing to do."

It's good that Columbus did not heed to criticism by his peers when he embarked upon the journey to discover India, and accidentally discovered America.

It's good that the Wright brothers did not give up due to nagging remarks by people such as, "Just do your work; forget about flying, only birds can fly;" otherwise the invention of the aeroplane would have still been a distant dream.

The first female bus driver was ridiculed, but she did not allow people's opinions to affect her. She paved the way for a whole new generation of female bus drivers.

Successful people like these did not stop due to fear of "what people will say" or fear of failure. They not only achieved success for themselves but also proved to be an inspiration for others.

All of the above methods will help you to transcend your fears. Instead of trying to escape from your fears or giving excuses, try these methods. It also helps to watch the fear meditatively. Observe what happens when you are fearful. Ask yourself, "Exactly what is happening?" Ask this question and observe your breath, your heart rate, and the sensations in the body. Watch as a detached witness. All these changes are occurring in your body-mind, not in you. You are simply the observer. Fear cannot touch you. Nothing can touch you. You are formless and limitless. With this perspective, fear no longer seems something insurmountable.

SUMMARY:

1. Actual failure is only when you stop trying. Unless you stop trying, you have not failed.
2. In spite of feeling fear, go ahead and do whatever you *can* do.
3. The best way to achieve freedom from fears is to face them.
4. By repeating positive and powerful affirmations every day, your life will be filled with fearlessness and courage.
5. Ignorance about failure creates fear about failure. Fear of failure attracts failure repeatedly. You can come out of this vicious cycle by focusing on success instead of failure.
6. Do what scientists do. On facing failure, try and change your method of working. By doing an old job in a new way, a new discovery can occur.
7. Failure is how *you think it to be*. If your perspective is right, failure is your teacher. Else, it is despair.
8. The feeling of 'I have' acts like a magnet and attracts the best towards you.
9. Instead of focusing on "what people will say," focus on "what's the right thing to do."
10. Observe what happens when you are fearful, and ask yourself, "Exactly what is happening?" You will realize that the symptoms of fear occur only on the body-mind. Nothing can touch you.

* * *

"You can be discouraged by failure, or you can learn from it.
So go ahead and make mistakes, make all you can.
Because, remember that's where you'll find success
—on the far side of failure."
— Thomas J. Watson

VOICE OF FAITH TO SHIFT FROM FAILURE TO SUCCESS

I believe in supreme life.
Thus, fear and insecurity are mere feelings that come and go.
I am safe.
It is safe to be successful.
Life loves me and wants me to succeed.
I handle my experiences with love, joy, and ease.
There is magic in my hands and words.
Every cell of my body is filled with the power of faith.
I am keen on letting this power manifest to its fullest.

Spiritual Secret 7

ANYTHING NEGATIVE IS AN ILLUSORY REALITY

*Behind the illusory reality
is the Truth and its attributes waiting to emerge.*

Beyond Positive and Negative thinking

Our thoughts are extremely powerful and have the ability to change our reality. When we generate or encourage negative thoughts, they begin to manifest through us. (The same applies to positive thoughts too). When we see negativity in others or in incidents, we attract more negativity in our life. Our feelings immediately become negative and we begin to create a negative reality for us. Being positive and thinking positively has always been suggested as the way to gain a new perspective towards unpleasant incidents; in helping us regain our balance and move ahead with life.

However, sometimes there is a flip side to this principle. Let us say you see a pricey car on the road, and instead of getting disheartened with the vehicle that you have, you think positively by saying, "I want to buy that car, and I can do it if I reach my financial goals." But when you look more deeply, you find beneath this positive thinking a subtle negative message: "I cannot afford that car right now." This negative feeling has an impact on you.

People always have questions like: "How can I think positively when my past has been scarred with negative incidents and failures? How can I generate positive thoughts? Even though I think positively, I am not able to make definitive changes in my life and I can't get out of the shell of negative feelings." Positive thinking is certainly better than negative thinking, but we have to add a new dimension to our thoughts in order to bring about a true change.

Is there a higher perspective or technique of relating to life situations that transcends the duality of negativity and positivity? Is it possible to maintain our level of consciousness even during negative circumstances like failures and create a new future? There is indeed: the solution lies in Truth Thinking. So, what is Truth Thinking?

When the sky is overcast, we see thick and ominous clouds that remind us of thunderstorms. However, if we were to raise ourselves above this blanket of clouds, we would witness the ever clear sky with bright sunshine. Truth Thinking is about remembering this higher perspective when the clouds of trials and tribulations loom over us in everyday life. Instead of worrying and complaining about challenging life situations or failures, we should confidently know that right behind these failures, success is knocking at our door.

All the negativity and limitations that we see around us—be it floods, droughts, a road accident, a financial crisis, a failure, disease, a relationship gone sour, or even something as commonplace as a traffic jam or bumpy road—these are nothing but the "illusory reality," something that appears real, but in fact is not so.

In such testing situations, one may be forced to think, "Life is so difficult. Something very bad is happening with me. Violence is on the rise. The government will never be effective. People are careless and selfish. If only my wife would change herself. Will I ever achieve success?..."

Indulging in such thinking, man is unaware of the Truth (the omnipresent Self, Source, Consciousness, God) that is waiting to be revealed behind this illusory reality; he is not conscious of the qualities of the Source that are waiting to be expressed. His thoughts based on illusory reality block new ideas and things from manifesting. How can anything be created unless seen first at the level of thoughts? When a person is busy in negative thinking, how can he even think of what he wants to create? Thoughts based on illusory reality keep him away from the innovations that are to be brought on to Earth for solving problems, for going beyond the challenges.

See every failure or rejection as an illusory reality. Never quit or give up. There have been instances where an individual commits suicide due to inability to find a job, and then an appointment letter arrives on the very same day. How unfortunate is that? Take inspiration from great personalities who did not give up despite numerous failures, such as Abraham Lincoln who lost in the elections 15 times before becoming the President, or Edison who failed in his experiments 10,000 times before succeeding in the invention of a viable electric bulb. Consider failure as an illusory reality and keep your focus on the success that is waiting behind to emerge.

In fact, you need to become a master of illusory reality by immediately identifying anything negative as an illusion. Instead of getting entangled in it and being trapped in the web of negative and limiting thoughts, you should train your focus on the hidden truth—the Source—that is ever-present in the background of these illusory scenes.

The Impact of Mass Media in the Shaping of Illusory Reality

Programming of our mind, positive as well as negative, takes place in our formative years by observing behavioral patterns around us.

This shapes our perception about life, joy, sorrow, success, failure, etc. and also about the world we live in. In addition, our perception of reality is also heavily influenced by mass media.

Mass media refers collectively to all means by which information reaches us. This includes the Internet, television, newspapers, and radio. Mass media plays a vital role in shaping public opinions on various issues, not only with the information that is dished out, but also through the particular interpretations of this information.

Negative content expressed by mass media makes viewers believe the world to be a more dangerous, hopeless, and miserable place. If we carefully scrutinize the effects of television on society, we will find that viewers who watch television indiscriminately tend to think of the world and life in general with skepticism and distrust. They tend to form skewed opinions and develop self-limiting attitudes. Mass media has a direct influence on how the viewer perceives the world as well as life.

Not until recently, our culture, our value system, and our understanding about life, success, or failure were shaped more by our parents, schools, and faith communities than by the influence of mass media. With the flourishing of newspapers, radio, television, and the internet, our perspective of reality is now shaped primarily by media corporations. They present a distorted perception of the world by focusing on a very limited part of world affairs. They define what is good and what is bad in life, what is success and what is failure, and we believe them. It is of the utmost importance that we learn and master the technique of Truth Thinking to be able to overcome this impact.

How to implement Truth Thinking

The Source is the creative principle; it's the source of all possibilities. Through Truth Thinking, we see the 'qualities of Source' instead of focusing on illusory reality. We welcome the shining sun, abundant harvest and ample food for all, cleanliness, compassion, love, courage, peace, patience, harmony, success, creativity—all of which are qualities of the Source. By allowing them to manifest, we invite these qualities into our lives, not only for us but for everyone around us. When we see these divine attributes hidden behind the illusion, we are released from our overwhelming negative feelings as well.

There are three steps for applying Truth Thinking:

Step 1: Tell yourself that this (negativity) is Illusory Reality

At the first step, you identify the present negative situation as illusory reality—which appears real, but isn't. However terrible the current situation may appear, you refuse to buy it. Even if someone is cursing you, or you have lost money in the stock market, or you are facing a failure in any aspect of your life, tell yourself, "This is an illusory reality." Thoughts like "What about my job? What's going to happen? People never change…" are all aspects of illusory reality. Even if you have fallen sick, identify it as an illusion. Good health is waiting at your doorstep. It wants to make an entry either with the help of a new cure, medicine, healing, or miracle. But it cannot manifest in your present reality if you refuse to see it. By not falling victim to the messages of illusory reality, you can invite all the best things into your life.

When you see and believe in illusions of life, you become like an element that attracts all that is negative. But when you choose to see the underlying Truth, you become a powerful magnet attracting all that is positive and highest. Only such people can bring new things onto Earth. One has to be undisturbed by the illusory reality to be able to see the Truth (the Source and all its divine attributes). If you get disturbed, you get carried away by illusion. Just by *identifying* the given situation as an illusory reality, you refuse to allow the situation to cast its spell on you.

Step 2: Access the heart to return to your original nature

In step two, you access your heart. The heart is the seat of your being, it's your center. By accessing the heart, you are able to reach the Source within you. This enables you to reaffirm the understanding that the Source is all around; that you are within it and it is within you. You realize at the experiential level that Source is the Truth and the situation you are facing is an illusion. When you experience this, you also realize that the Source is teeming with infinite possibilities. You become aware of your true potential. If you fall under the spell of illusory reality, you fail to understand your true potential. You become a victim and shrink into limitations. When you access the Source, you remember your true nature, which is characterized by boundless love, unbroken peace, supreme joy, and limitless possibilities.

Step 3: Invoke the quality of Source through gratitude

In step three, you invoke a certain quality of the Source by saying "Thank You for _____.' You have to invoke that particular quality which is the opposite of the negative that you are experiencing. When you express gratitude to the Source, you are honoring whatever you are being grateful for, thereby allowing it to manifest in your reality.

For example, when you go out for a walk and notice something negative, like a wall spoiled by graffiti, identify it as illusory reality. Tell yourself, "Everything on Earth is a piece of creativity and I am here to see the best creations. Thank You for creativity." Creativity is one of the qualities of the Source. By doing this, you are invoking this particular quality, and sowing the seeds that will subsequently germinate. Along the same lines, if you are facing a failure or a setback, say to the Source, "Thank You for success." Success is also an attribute of the Source; it will be invoked and will subsequently manifest in your life.

Does this mean that you should remain passive? Not at all. You have to take the best action befitting the situation. If you are stuck in a traffic jam, find the best way out. The moment you say "Thank You for smoothness," you give direction to the positive energies of the universe, which in turn help you to find the best way out and make your journey smooth.

If someone is behaving rudely with you, the moment you say "Thank You for peace and harmony," you are invoking peace and harmony within yourself and the other person. Their behavior towards you is bound to change. If you consistently invoke these divine qualities within them, they may change forever! Even a single utterance of gratitude can trigger the process of change.

Truth Thinking—A Technique for Definitive Change

When you focus only on illusory reality, you entangle and constrict the universal powers and create the wrong things in your reality. Truth thinking is not a temporary feel-good solution. It is a dynamic technique to bring about definitive change. This method can break down all the limitations in your thinking. When you say 'Thank You for…' you are sending a signal to the universe that you see only the Truth and thereby the entire universe rallies behind you. Divine qualities start working through you. Nature signals you about the change that has begun through your feeling—you can witness the change in your feeling from negative to positive.

Truth thinking is not merely a practice of positive thinking or imaging. Positive thinking can often lead to negative thinking. Truth thinking is a higher practice of seeing the Truth. It focuses on reaching your original essence through gratitude for the divine qualities of the Source. When you see good in others, say, "Thank You for goodness," "Thank You for perfection," "Thank You for timely help," "Thank You for all the divine qualities." This will enhance the goodness and divinity in your life.

When you see any negativity as an illusory reality and instead choose to see the underlying qualities of the Source, those qualities manifest abundantly in your life. The Source has created everything in the world in abundance. That's right! Everything you could possibly need or want has already been created for you; regardless of the present appearance of your life, which is simply an illusion. The truth is love, peace, bliss, success, health, and wealth have been created abundantly and are flowing freely towards each and every one in the world.

You may wonder, "If this is true, then why do we see so much poverty and misery on Earth? Why isn't everyone experiencing abundance?" That is because: *You naturally progress towards your highest potential in life, so long as you do not place obstacles in the free flow from the Source.*

The obstacles are negative thinking, negative feeling, limiting beliefs, and focusing on the illusory reality. These are like blocks that clog the pipe through which abundance is flowing towards you. When you remove these blocks, the free flow of abundance begins in your life. When you have unwavering faith in the Truth (the Source) and deep conviction that everything is flowing freely in your life, then you become receptive to abundance. So, from the depth of your heart, say to the Source, "Thank You for abundance—of health, wealth, love, joy, and peace."

SUMMARY:

1. If there is a negative feeling behind positive thinking, then it prevents positive results.

2. Instead of worrying about challenging life situations or failures, we should confidently know that right behind these failures, success is knocking at our door.

3. All the negativity and limitations that we see around us are nothing but the "illusory reality," something that appears real, but in fact is not so.

4. Indulging in negative thinking, man is unaware of the Source and its attributes that are waiting to emerge behind this illusory reality.

5. Just by identifying a negative situation as an illusory reality, you refuse to allow the situation to cast its spell on you.

6. When you access the Source, you remember your true nature, which is characterized by boundless love, unbroken peace, supreme joy, and limitless possibilities.

7. You invoke a certain quality of the Source by saying "Thank You for ____." You have to invoke that particular quality which is the opposite of the negative that you are experiencing.

8. When you say "Thank You for ____" you are sending a signal to the universe that you see only the Truth and thereby the entire universe rallies behind you.

9. You naturally progress toward your highest potential in life, so long as you do not place obstacles in the free flow from the Source.

10. Truth Thinking is beyond positive and negative thinking; it focuses on reaching your original essence through gratitude for the divine qualities of the Source.

* * *

Luminous Lives

NELSON MANDELA

> "It always seems impossible until it's done."
> – Nelson Mandela

Nelson Mandela is well known throughout the world as the first black President of South Africa. He played a major role in liberating his country from the curse of apartheid and bringing an end to the unrest caused by racism. He was imprisoned for 27 years and his whole life was dedicated to the fight for freedom from racism. The Nobel Peace Prize in 1993 was awarded jointly to Nelson Mandela and Frederik Willem de Klerk "for their work for the peaceful termination of the apartheid regime and for laying the foundations for a new, democratic South Africa."

Early life

Rolihlahla Mandela was born in a village of South Africa on July 18, 1918. His father was a local chief who was sacked from his job by the colonial authorities. Both his parents were illiterate, but being a devout Christian, his mother sent him to a local Methodist school when he was about seven. Baptized in his school, Mandela was given the English forename of "Nelson" by his teacher. After he lost his father at the tender age of nine, he went through various experiences, schools, and jobs that exposed him to the suffering of the native people due to racial discrimination by the white government.

Politics, Prison, Leadership

Nelson Mandela became increasingly involved in politics in his youth. "I saw that it was not just my freedom that was curtailed, but the freedom of everyone who looked like I did." His hunger for his own freedom became the greater hunger for the freedom of his people. This transformed a frightened young man into a bold one. He participated in various boycotts and strikes against apartheid. He fought for equality, right to education, right to property, and rights for laborers. He was repeatedly arrested for his rebellious activities. Although initially committed to non-violent protest, in 1961 he led a sabotage campaign against the government. In 1962, he was arrested for "conspiring to overthrow the state," and sentenced to life imprisonment.

He spent 27 years in jail. His prison life was extremely hard. He also suffered from tuberculosis due to the damp conditions in his cell, in addition to innumerable other problems. His mother and his son died when he was in jail but he was forbidden from attending either funeral.

As he recalls, "There were many dark moments when my faith in humanity was sorely tested, but I would not and could not give myself up to despair." It was during those long and lonely years that his hunger for the freedom of his people became a hunger for the freedom of all people, black and white. After all, a man who takes away another man's freedom is also a prisoner of hatred and prejudice. And therefore, despite every adversity, he continued the movement against racial discrimination as well as his L.L.B. studies (whenever he was allowed) during his imprisonment.

His life in jail with silent suffering and quiet protest proved to be highly inspirational for people of his country as well as other nations. Many people and organizations around the world rallied in various ways for his release from prison. He had become the world's most famous prisoner, a symbol of the anti-apartheid cause, and an icon for millions who embraced the ideal of human equality. After suffering for so many years, he was finally released in February 1990. He says, "As I walked toward the gate that would lead to my freedom, I knew if I did not leave my bitterness and hatred behind, I would still be in prison..."

With this thought, he chose forgiveness and not resentment or retribution. This is because he believed that one can achieve more in this world through acts of mercy than through acts of retribution. He also knew that holding on to resentment is like drinking poison and then hoping it will kill one's enemies. Hence he let go of all negative feelings and left his prison with a clear mission—to liberate the oppressed and the oppressor both.

From his life in prison he had learned that to be free is not merely to cast off one's chains, but to live in a way that respects and enhances the freedom of others. Therefore he proceeded on a tour to various parts of Africa and other countries around the world to encourage them to support sanctions against the apartheid government.

Thereafter he negotiated with the then President of South Africa, and both of them together successfully brought an end to apartheid and also organized a multiracial general election in 1994. Mandela won in the elections and became the country's first black head of state and the first elected in a fully representative democratic election. His government focused on dismantling the legacy of apartheid by tackling institutionalized racism and fostering racial reconciliation. He created a commission to investigate past human rights abuses and introduced measures to encourage land reform, combat poverty and illiteracy, and expand healthcare services.

He declined a second presidential term and instead focused on charitable work through the *Nelson Mandela Foundation*. In 2007, he established an NGO called *The Elders* in which he brought together independent global leaders to work for peace and human rights. Their goal is to work on solutions for overwhelming global problems like HIV/AIDS, climate change, human rights, and poverty.

Mandela passed away in 2013, in Johannesburg. His vision was great and so were his actions. His attitude towards life was: "There is no passion to be found playing small—in settling for a life that is less than the one you are capable of living." People all over the globe acknowledged that the true tribute to him would be to follow his noble principles of toleration, liberal democracy, and social justice.

Teachings from Mandela's life

Throughout his life, Mandela worked for the society as a youth leader and then as a politician, due to which he was imprisoned multiple times. He stuck to his principles even during imprisonment and that is why people trusted him. Even though his opponents tried to bring him down by various means, he became very popular and powerful due to his undying commitment to a noble cause.

Mandela never gave in to situations and rose back after every setback. This is because he knew the greatest glory in living lies not in never falling, but in rising every time we fall. He persevered relentlessly even in the face of highly challenging and grave circumstances. It's not like he never felt fear, but he overcame it because he believed, "Courage is not the absence of fear, but the triumph over it. The brave man is not he who does not feel afraid, but he who conquers that fear."

With his total dedication to an impersonal cause, he was successful in combating every obstacle and every failure. His life exemplified his belief: "What counts in life is not the mere fact that we have lived. It is what difference we have made to the lives of others." He is the epitome of forgiveness, courage, and perseverance.

• • •

SECTION II

7 STEPS TO SHIFT FROM FAILURE TO SUPREME SUCCESS

Step 1

VOICE OF FAITH

What is true for God, is true for me.

Let's perform an experiment. There may be both successful and unsuccessful people around you—at home, at work, among your relatives, or among your friends. Observe both kinds of people and listen to the words that emerge from their mouth all day. You will find an unmistakable difference in the speech and tone of the two kinds of people.

Successful people commonly use positive words, while unsuccessful people mostly use negative words. Successful people are generally upbeat and have a great attitude, while unsuccessful people are usually unhappy and have a pessimistic attitude. Words of successful people typically ooze confidence, while unsuccessful people often speak tentatively, apprehensively, angrily, sadly, or plain negatively. Successful people usually don't hesitate to appreciate others and speak good things about them, while unsuccessful people always seek to attract everyone's attention to themselves. Successful people normally speak about everyone, while unsuccessful people habitually speak about themselves and most of their sentences are full of 'I', 'me', 'my' or 'mine'. Successful people more often than not give others the credit for their victories, while unsuccessful people often try to steal all the credit from others.

You can find a definite pattern in the speech of highly successful people and highly unsuccessful people. Now record your speech for a whole day if possible, from morning to night. Listen to the recording. What do you come to know about yourself? What are your words like? Are they like successful people, like unsuccessful people, or something in between? This experiment will give you a jolt. It will awaken you to your present condition. Today you have to make a decision—the decision to change the way you speak, for this is the first step towards ultimate success.

Our words empower our thoughts and turn them into reality. Whether your condition today is good or bad, the words you spoke, the thoughts you chose to empower, have played a crucial role in it.

All types of thoughts run through our mind all day—godly as well as individual-centric, good as well as bad, positive as well as negative, optimistic as well as pessimistic. Which type of thoughts are we choosing to speak? Which kind of feeling are we evoking in ourselves? A great law of nature is at work here—the Law of Focus, due to which *whatever you focus on, grows in your life*. The words we use throughout the day create powerful vibrations that program our subconscious mind to attract similar things in our life through the law of focus.

If our words are so powerful, wouldn't we like to use only the purest, best, and most positive words that we can think of? Wouldn't we want to empower only the godly thoughts that run through our mind? Powerful and divine thoughts are constantly emerging from our supreme self (the Self, the Source, or God) and passing through our mind. We are meant to act upon them in order to lead a grand and blissful life. The Self (or God) has created us to express itself and its divine qualities through our body. It wants each one of us to attain our highest potential. It is taking care of each of us. The Self wants to express itself through our body. If we are not successful in life, it means we are failing to catch godly thoughts and lend them our words.

All we need to do to identify godly thoughts is to raise our awareness. Then it is easy to separate godly thoughts from individual-centric thoughts. Just think: if you get a thought that you are miserable and helpless, is this is a godly thought or an individual-centric thought? Obviously, an individual-centric one. God can never feel miserable or helpless, only the individual can. If you feel like criticizing someone, blaming or wishing bad for someone, this is an individual-centric thought. If you feel like wishing well for someone, praying for someone, or seeking forgiveness for someone, this is a godly thought. If you feel like satisfying your own selfish desires, this is an individual-centric thought. If you feel like doing good for everyone around you, this is a godly thought. If you wish to crush others in order to succeed, this is an individual-centric thought. If you wish that everyone succeeds and progresses together, this is a godly thought. If you doubt your own abilities, this is an individual-centric thought. If you think God resides within you and God's abilities are supreme, this is a godly thought. If you feel suspicious, insecure, scared, jealous, or hateful, these are individual-centric thoughts. If you feel that the same limitless Self is expressing through everyone and hence there is nothing to fear or hate, this is a godly thought.

When you think godly thoughts, you get a happy and expansive feeling, because those thoughts are perfectly aligned with your essence. On the other hand, whenever you think individual-centric thoughts, God or Self instantly sends you a message in the form of a bad feeling. This is to convey that what you are thinking about yourself or others is not aligned with your true nature. He wants to remind you the truth, "You are my descendant... you are part of me... you are me. You have the same powers and attributes that I have."

Thus you see that it is easy to discern godly thoughts from individual-centric thoughts. Every human being on Earth gets godly thoughts because God resides within everyone—it's just that most people choose to ignore them in favour of individual-centric thoughts. We rarely listen to His voice. Rather, we don't even know or believe that God talks to us. The more you ignore godly thoughts, the less you get them. It is important to choose which kind of thoughts to empower through our words. Giving a voice to godly thoughts creates a magic potion, while giving a voice to individual-centric thoughts creates poison.

So, whenever you experience self-pity and associated bad feelings, remind yourself to welcome godly thoughts and ask yourself, "How does God see me? Helpless...? Worthless...?" Of course not! God never sees anybody this way. The bad feelings that you experience are, firstly, a message from God that you are not thinking according to your true nature. Secondly, those bad feelings are a push from God to break the limitations of the individual-centric mind and think higher. Otherwise, man stuck in comforts and conveniences doesn't make an effort by himself to take the next leap of faith until God pushes him through these negative feelings. It is when he gets tired of negative feelings that he decides to break through self-imposed limitations and progress ahead.

Thus, to move from failure to ultimate success, you must first of all choose to give voice to godly thoughts. This voice is the VOICE OF FAITH. 'Faith' here indicates you *believe* that your true nature is divine and all-powerful, and therefore when you utter something, it *has to* come true. Voice of faith is thus a magic potion that you don't have to drink with your mouth but *produce* with your mouth. Always remember: WHAT IS TRUE FOR GOD, IS TRUE FOR ME.

Some people may not be able to believe that their real nature is divine. Depending on your level of faith, you may believe either of the following:

- You are a part of Divinity.
- The Divine resides within you.
- You are a creation of the Divine. Hence God wants the best and highest for you.

You can then give voice to your faith accordingly. For example: If you believe that your real nature is divine, you will say, "I am Success. Success is my nature." If you believe God resides within you, then God says, "I am Success. Success is my nature." So, you will give voice to this thought. If you believe you are a creation of God, you will say, "I am God's property. Hence God is helping me to succeed. My success is assured."

The voice of faith will help in the manifestation of anything you want: love, joy, peace, total health, abundance... In fact, the more faith you have, the more success you can achieve. Otherwise, you may have seen that there are many people who have a lot of talent and skills but are unable to attain success. But a complete transformation is possible when you give voice to God's thoughts. You will start seeing miracles. As soon as you express a divine thought, you get a good feeling. Even though the problem may be still standing before you, the good feeling will give you the conviction that the problem will soon go away. The solution is created as soon as you use the voice of faith, it's just that it will take some time for it to appear in the physical plane. This is the power of voice of faith. It gets things moving in the invisible plane.

Problems that appear in our life are a result of our own belief system. By constantly speaking individual-centric thoughts, we start believing that we are a limited individual, thus inviting a plethora of individual related problems. The truth is that our body is simply a form of the formless and infinite God. The formless and infinite divinity is our true nature, our true self. We need to voice the qualities of our true self. Our true self is all-powerful, omnipotent, unconditionally loving, unconditionally happy, peaceful, compassionate, courageous, patient, and all-pervading. Most importantly, our true self is merely a witness of all that is happening with our body-mind and the world around us. It is only the individual that gets sucked up in incidents happening with the body-mind.

This knowledge of our true self and its qualities is gained by the grace of a true spiritual master, through the medium of spiritual discourses or books. The master is the messenger of God. When the thoughts stop coming from God due to habitually ignoring them, it is the grace of the master that revives those godly thoughts. None other than a truly self-realized and self-stabilized master can impart to us the wisdom of our true self.

As soon as we produce the magic potion with our voice of faith, its impact begins. It bestows immense benefits on the body and mind. It boosts physical and mental health. It boosts immunity, the power to repel illnesses. The magic potion repels not just physical ailments but also mental ones like sadness, bitterness, hatred, jealousy, etc.

Hence start producing the magic potion with your mouth. Start uttering the voice of faith. Speak as Divinity or give voice to Divinity residing within you. (And this is how it differs from affirmations.) Whenever you feel sad, say to yourself, "Happiness is my nature. I AM HAPPINESS." Or if you believe God resides within you, what will God say if you are feeling unhappy? He will probably say, "I have made man in my image to experience and express happiness. I AM HAPPINESS." Give voice to these words, feel them, and speak them out mentally or aloud: "I am made in the image of God to experience and express happiness. I am happy. I AM HAPPINESS."

This will detach you from the incident causing the unhappiness as well as from that feeling.

Similarly, if you are feeling unloved, either say, "I love everyone and everyone loves me. I AM LOVE," or lend your voice to God's thought: "I am made in the image of God to experience and express love. I AM LOVE." Speak this out and allow love to permeate your heart.

If you are feeling restless, irritated, or angry, say, "I let go of all the thoughts that I don't need. I AM PEACE," or lend your voice to God's thought: "I am made in the image of God to experience and express peace. I AM PEACE."

If you are troubled by ill-health, proclaim: "God cannot be sick; so how can I? I AM HEALTH. My face radiates health and vitality. Divine energy is coursing through every cell of my body."

If you have fallen ill because of neglecting signs of an ailment, seek forgiveness and say, "I love and respect my body. I am sorry for having neglected it for so long. Henceforth I shall take good care of it."

If you get feelings of lack of any kind, including money, assert to yourself: "Everything is abundant in the universe. ABUNDANCE IS MY NATURE. Abundance is constantly flowing in my life."

Whenever you feel scared, anxious, or insecure, say to yourself, "Fear, anxiety, and insecurity are merely thoughts that pass through the mind. I am not the body or the mind. I am the master of my body-mind, not its slave. COURAGE IS MY NATURE."

Whenever you feel afraid of failure, say, "This task may look difficult, but it is not difficult for the divine power of God." Remind yourself, "Difficult tasks are meant for increasing the capability of the body-mind. Increased capability leads to better Self Expression."

If you are feeling dejected due to a setback or failure, proclaim: "God cannot fail; so how can I? This failure is a ladder towards supreme success. I am destined to succeed because SUCCESS IS MY NATURE."

To overcome fear of mistakes, tell yourself, "Mistakes help the body-mind to grow. I accept whatever mistakes are made and learn from them. I let go of the fear of making mistakes."

If you are low on self-esteem, proclaim your divinity: "I know how important and extraordinary I am. I am unlimited, all-knowing, and all-pervasive."

To get rid of guilt and self-hatred, say, "I forgive my body for all that it did in the past. I am releasing all that is now unnecessary. I AM FREE. I AM FREEDOM."

If you are subdued due to low self-confidence, say to yourself, "NOTHING IS IMPOSSIBLE FOR THE SUPREME SELF. There is nothing that I cannot do. I allow myself to move ahead."

Inspiration for such thoughts will come from various sources—spiritual discourses, spiritual and self-help books and videos, and even from friends, family, and colleagues. You will instantly know which thought is godly and which is not. The thought that expands your heart and generates a generous feeling in you is godly. Your duty is to catch hold of godly thoughts and voice them.

Use the voice of faith not just with yourself but also when interacting with others. When someone asks you, "How are you?" always respond with "Good!" or "Great!" Even if you are feeling low, this voice of faith will remind you of your true nature, which is always "great." Always encourage others and never let anyone's enthusiasm drop because of what you say. Be a source of inspiration to others. People should feel good when they see you. Their faces should not droop on seeing you. You should take care to speak only positive words especially when you are with your family, as it is easy to turn sad and bitter when you are with your own people. Don't make your near-and-dear ones lose their level of consciousness.

After reading the voice of faith statements, your mind may say, "No, this cannot be true. If I am not feeling good, how can I say that I am great? If I am sick, how can I say that I am healthy? Is this not lying?" This question can be best answered with the help of a story.

A thief sneaked into a priest's house to hide from the police. The priest saw him and treated him like a guest. He let him stay in his house for a few days. Before leaving, the thief pocketed a gold lamp from the worship room. A few days later, the thief was caught. The police found the gold lamp in his possession. Their investigation led them to the priest's home. When they asked the priest if the lamp belonged to him, the priest said, "I gave this lamp to this man as a gift. He was my guest for a few days." Since the police could not find any other evidence against the thief, they let him go.

After the police left, the thief turned to the priest and expressed his gratitude. He said, "Thank you for saving me from imprisonment. But I have a question. Why did you lie even though you are a priest?"

The priest replied, "I lied because I have faith that this is your last theft."

The thief was moved. For the first time, someone had placed so much faith in him. Indeed, he stopped stealing and turned to good ways to earn a living. The priest's voice of faith won, even though it seemed like a lie.

Thus, the voice of faith is never a lie; it is in fact the supreme truth. Even if it seems like a lie, it will put a full stop to the problems that are troubling you. It is a great power. It is faith in the unseen higher possibility; faith in something divine that is yet to manifest in the physical form. People go to great lengths to develop faith. They undertake penance, visit holy shrines walking on foot for hundreds of miles, perform lengthy rituals as proposed by holy men, and so on. But this faith can be developed sitting at home as well. All you need to do is start voicing your faith in godly thoughts.

Usually when people run into problems or feel low, they resort to watching comedy shows on television, drinking, shopping, meeting up and chatting with friends, etc. They get temporary relief from their negative feeling but this is not a solution. It's like digging a second pit to fill up the emptiness of the first pit. The only permanent method to fill the emptiness inside us is to infuse our entire being with the voice of faith. This voice connects us back to the Source (God, Self)—the unending supply of positivity, love, joy, and peace.

Let the voice of faith permeate every cell, every nerve, muscle, bone, and even the bone marrow of your body. Just like threads of wool are interwoven to make a sweater, interweave the voice of faith with every cell of your body. Knit it so thoroughly that it never comes loose or comes off. Let faith in divine thoughts make a permanent residence in your mind and body. Then no matter what happens or what people say to you, your divinity will not diminish one bit. Nothing will be able to disturb you or lower your level of consciousness. Negative incidents may happen around you, people may blame or criticize you, people may give you bad news, your kid may fall sick, you may encounter failure… No matter what happens, your optimism, positivity, faith, love, joy, and peace will be maintained.

So, take benefit of this amazing technique to overcome the feeling of failure and move towards ultimate success. Your focus plays a critical role in your life. It will take you either to the pinnacle of success or to the depths of failure. It's your choice where to go. No matter how many problems and difficulties come your way, if your focus is upwards, you will move upwards. When you start seeing the results of your voice of faith, your speed of progress will increase tremendously because of receiving proof that this technique works.

Speak up to strengthen your focus. Proclaim what kind of health you want at the physical level, what kind of wellbeing you want at the mental level, what kind of love you want at the social level, what kind of prosperity you want at the financial level, and what kind of liberation you want at the spiritual level. Your words will help to manifest all that you want in life. This is not a form of affirmation or auto-suggestion or an attempt to change your self talk. It is having faith in the highest and verbalizing what the Supreme Self wants to say.

The more negative your focus today, the more magic potion you will need to produce with your mouth. Decide your dosage and begin. Continue producing the magic potion until you reach the final state of success—freedom from the sense of individuality and becoming who you actually are—the Supreme Self. Then, you won't need to say anything, you'll just be.

SUMMARY:

1. All kinds of thoughts pass through our mind all day long. Most thoughts are individual-centric, while some are godly.

2. If we speak individual-centric thoughts, we immediately get a negative feeling, because those thoughts create poison. On the other hand, if we speak godly thoughts, it creates a feel-good magic potion which is the cure for all kinds of failure.

3. If we raise our awareness and remain a detached witness to the thoughts passing through our mind, it is easy to differentiate between godly thoughts and other thoughts. In order to progress towards success, we need to give our voice to godly thoughts—the voice of faith.

4. Words empower thoughts and strengthen focus, this is what helps attract whatever we want in life.

5. There is no need to fight negative and individual-centric thoughts. Our only job is to empower godly thoughts with our voice. All that remains then is to wait and watch with wonder.

6. All that we want—physical health, mental wellbeing, emotional balance, financial prosperity, spiritual liberation, love, joy, peace—can be achieved with the power of the voice of faith.

7. The voice of faith connects us to our divinity. In that state, failure does not exist. We realize that God cannot fail, so how can I?

8. What is true for God, is true for me.

9. Speak as Divinity or the Self, because that is who you are.

10. Let the voice of faith permeate every cell, every nerve, muscle, bone, and even the bone marrow of your body. This will help you become who you really are and achieve your grandest vision.

* * *

"If even one person in the world can do something,
you can do it too."

— Sirshree

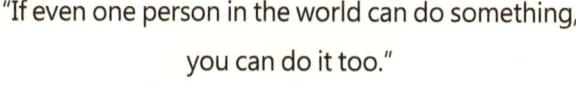

PRAYER

TO CONNECT TO THE SELF

I am made in the image of God.

Peace is the nature of God; hence peace is spreading within me.

Waves of joy are arising all around me.

I am feeling calm and serene.

Anger, problems, and worries may hover over me,

yet I am peaceful, assured, and stable.

Peace... Peace... Peace...

STEP 2

INSPIRED ACTION

*Actions inspired by the Self
result in the best creations and extraordinary success.*

After giving voice to the thoughts emerging from the Self, let's see what is the next step.

Once Albert Einstein, the famous scientist, used a $1500 cheque as a bookmark. The funny thing is, after he finished reading the book, he threw the cheque in the dustbin assuming it to be a bookmark. He was so absorbed in his work that nothing distracted him.

Similarly, once the Jain writer Pandit Todarmal was engrossed in writing a book, which later became popular under the title *Moksha Marg* (The Path to Liberation). As soon as he would wake up in the morning, he would resume writing the book with full concentration and continue until late at night. He was not aware of the world around him, neither did he care about food or anything else. This continued for many days. He was completely devoted to this work and put his heart and soul into it.

After some months, while having a meal he told his mother, "Mother, I think today you forgot to add salt in the vegetable dish." His mother remarked, "Son, it seems you have finished writing the book." Todarmal was astonished because his mother's guess was absolutely correct. He said, "Yes, Mother. You're right. Today I have completed the book. But how did you know?" His mother replied with a smile, "My son, for the last six months I have NOT been adding salt in the food, but you never noticed because you were absorbed in the book. Today when you noticed it, I realized that now you can think about food, so you must have finished the book."

Such actions happen only with inner inspiration. These can be called as inspired karma.

Inspired Karma

There are thoughts that emerge from the Source or Self (some may call it thoughts emerging from the heart). When we act on these thoughts, we experience complete fulfillment. The Self is continuously giving us such thoughts. The actions that follow such thoughts are called 'inspired karma.' You need to tune yourself to inner inspiration and perform inspired karma. Such karma not only give you the feeling of fulfillment but also lead you towards the best creations and amazing success.

Suppose a child is sitting in his room and suddenly he gets a thought: "I will make a paper boat." He jumps up and runs off to find a sheet of paper. He then learns how to make a paper boat, and makes one. With joy and vigor he teaches the technique to other kids as well. He happily lets the boat float in a stream of water. He spends an hour or two playing with it. He enjoys it so much because he acted on the inspiration that arose from the Self. A single thought became a cause of joy for all the kids. This is what inspired karma is. Such actions, done with vigor and agility, become a source of inspiration... not only for the doer but for many others as well.

In this example the boy was engaged in inspired action for one or two hours. However, you may find at times that you are inspired to carry out an action that takes several hours to complete. You may easily spend many hours on it, and may not even notice how time flew by.

Some more examples of inspired karma are:

- A housewife gets a thought of making a new dish and immediately begins the preparation. Actions emerge with such ease that within no time the dish is ready. Even she wonders how she could have made that dish so effortlessly when she otherwise takes a lot of time to prepare any dish. This act is inspired karma.

- A poet is in the shower. Some verses emerge from his heart. These later get composed into a song and people hum this song for years to come. This is the magic of inspiration.

- The scientific inventions that have been made on this planet are nothing but a result of inspired karma.

- Melodious hymns, poems, beautiful stories, and other works of art are the creative expressions of inspired karma.

- A person is thinking about cleaning his house since many days but cannot get down to it because he dislikes cleaning. One day he is struck by a thought of inspired action, and within no time his house is spick and span. How could the activity he disliked be completed so easily? This is because inspired karma has immense power. Such action is supported by the power of feeling. In fact, inspired karma plays a major role in the completion of any work that gets done on Earth.

Thoughts of inspired action emerge from the Self. Such actions take place in a spontaneous manner, without a sense of doer-ship or feeling of doing. They just happen. This is what is meant by inspired karma.

If you consistently act on the inspiration that flows from within at every stage of life, you will flow freely in the river of life. This will lead you to success in every aspect. That's not all. It will also help you to achieve the purpose of your life.

Free Flow Sadhana

So, how do you shift from negative feelings of failure to inspired karma? By regarding failure as an illusory reality and performing Free Flow Sadhana. We have learnt about the 'illusory reality' in previous chapters, where we understood that anything negative that we see is actually an illusion, although it appears to be real. In order to overcome the illusory reality, one needs to practice dispassion. You can remain dispassionate by performing Free Flow Sadhana.

One may assume that *sadhana* (spiritual practice) means abstaining from society and sitting in meditation in a cave or a forest. However, sadhana actually means achieving the ultimate purpose of life while performing your everyday duties, and expressing the divine qualities of God, like love, joy, and peace. According to the principle of Free Flow, *everything that is of your highest interest is naturally flowing in your life.* Being gracefully present in this flow is Free Flow Sadhana. Life goes on, one incident after the other, in its natural flow. Simply be present in this free flow, with purity of mind and a feeling of abundance.

Free Flow Sadhana means reaching the destination smoothly. When the mind becomes steadfast in every event, life becomes fluid; the thoughts and emotions that surface begin to become fluid. With this sadhana you learn to accept every event gracefully, because of the conviction that everything that is happening is for your highest good. In this fluidity, one attains ultimate success as well as the ultimate purpose of life.

There are two ways to live: either you try to swim upstream against the force of the river, or you move along with the flow and surrender to its fluidity. The river of life is taking you to your destination; Free Flow Sadhana is when you flow with life without any resistance.

When your thoughts and feelings become fluid, you are in a 'no-resistance' state. You don't resist anything because you identify whatever is happening as 'illusory reality' and watch it dispassionately.

If you read the biographies of great people, you will come to know about the problems and setbacks that occurred in their lives. Despite those calamities and failures, they were able to maintain their inner peace. This is sadhana.

Some may misunderstand Free Flow Sadhana as sitting idly and doing nothing to improve their present state. They need to understand the real meaning of it. In this sadhana, spontaneous actions or inspired karma happen through you that improve your present, because there is no unnecessary chattering of your mind. When the mind frets and dwells on problems or failures, it does not allow the free flow to work in your life. It blocks the natural flow. Sadhana quiets the mind and removes these blocks. Most of the people on this planet try to solve problems while they are fretting within. Fretting makes every problem to become a burden, and resolving it becomes more difficult. On the contrary, Free Flow Sadhana resolves problems effortlessly because you get inspiration from within regarding what needs to be understood and what needs to be done. Such inspired karma will shift you from the feeling of failure towards growth and higher success.

When your mind chatters—saying things like, "Why did God give me so many setbacks?" or "Why me?"—tell your mind, "This is that what I need, so that I can learn to overcome challenges and achieve big success." Practice this sadhana for every complaint that your mind makes. If you find someone criticizing you behind your back, you feel hurt. Identify this as an opportunity to practice Free Flow Sadhana. In this scenario, tell yourself, "Whatever the person is thinking about me is just feedback for me. It is the necessity of this moment. This is what I need now." And if that feedback does not have any substance, don't allow it to impact you negatively.

Abide in a state of happiness, wonder, and praise of the Self, believing that your voice of faith and prayer is coming true. Otherwise, everything—love, health, wealth, success—that was coming towards you gets stuck somewhere. As soon as you shift to the above-mentioned wonderful feelings, everything starts moving towards you again. Shifting to those feelings is actual Free Flow Sadhana.

Now that you understand the importance of Free Flow Sadhana, marvel at this manifestation process and leave your worries aside. Enjoy the present moment. Be child-like—always in the feeling of wonderment. Repenting the past or worrying about the future drains energy from the present, making you weak, lethargic, and tired. On the contrary, when you practice living in the present, you save your energy, and with this energy the next step of transformation unfolds.

Transformation occurs when you get higher thoughts. Though material success is important, but success of the mission with which you have come to Earth is more important. According to the principle of Free Flow, the Self will keep giving you thoughts of your higher interest like, "Why am I here? Why is my body here?" These thoughts lead you to achieve your purpose of being on this planet. As you continue to perform inspired karma, you will receive answers for these questions, and your ultimate purpose becomes clearer. This is the power of inspiration.

When the mind is calm and relaxed, we can catch the thoughts that arise from the Self. Everyone receives thoughts of inspired karma, because the Self resides within everyone. Everyone is here on Earth to carry out creative and supreme work. If you are a doctor, then recognize the thoughts of inspired karma so that you become a great doctor and serve your patients in the best possible way. You may be a teacher, engineer, artist, lawyer, student, or a writer. Whatever your field, you can reach the heights of success in your field, provided you recognize the thoughts of inspired karma and act on them to turn them into physical reality.

Inspired karma is one of the main principles of transformation. It is inspired action that transformed an ordinary student to "Einstein," Narendra to "Swami Vivekananda," and Mohandas Karamchand Gandhi to "Mahatma Gandhi." Inspired action can transform an ordinary sportsman to a world famous athlete, or an ordinary housewife to a successful businesswoman.

The Uniqueness of Inspired Karma

There is a difference between ordinary actions and inspired actions. The following points elucidate the uniqueness of inspired karma:

- In most cases inspiration or thoughts of inspired karma appear suddenly when they are least expected. We can catch these thoughts when our conscious mind is calm and relaxed.
- One does not get physically or mentally tired while performing inspired karma.
- During inspired karma, the conscious mind is calm, enthusiastic, and joyful.
- When one acts on inspired karma, one experiences feelings of wonderment and fulfillment at the work one has accomplished.
- When one performs inspired karma with the right understanding, there won't be the slightest thought or feeling of doer-ship.

Many people don't understand inspiration, or intuition: the tuition that occurs from within. When you pray or practice voice of faith, you will find that thoughts of inspired karma start occurring.

Contemplate how your life could be if every action of yours was inspired karma!

What should you do until you get thoughts of inspired karma? You must practice the next step, which is 'developing capability'.

SUMMARY:

1. Tune yourself to inner inspiration and perform inspired karma. Such karma will not only give you the feeling of fulfillment but also lead you towards the best creations and amazing success.

2. When you pray or practice voice of faith, you will find that thoughts of inspired karma start occurring.

3. Inspired actions, done with vigor and agility, become a source of inspiration… not only for the doer but for many others as well.

4. The scientific inventions that have taken place on this planet are nothing but a result of inspired karma.

5. Melodious hymns, poems, beautiful stories, and other works of art are the creative expressions of inspired karma.

6. Inspired karma plays a major role in the completion of any work that gets done on Earth.

7. If you consistently act on the inspiration that flows from within, at every stage of life, you will flow freely in the river of life. This will lead you to success in every aspect. That's not all. It will also help you to achieve the purpose of your life.

8. According to the principle of Free Flow, *everything that is of your highest interest is naturally flowing in your life.*

9. The river of life is taking you to your destination; Free Flow Sadhana is when you flow with life without any resistance.

10. Free Flow Sadhana resolves problems effortlessly because you get inspiration from within regarding what needs to be understood and what needs to be done. Such inspired karma will shift you from the feeling of failure towards growth and higher success.

* * *

Luminous Lives

HELEN KELLER

"*Optimism is the faith that leads to achievement. Nothing can be done without hope and confidence.*"
— Helen Keller

Helen Keller was an American author, political activist, and lecturer. She overcame the adversity of being blind and deaf to become one of the leading humanitarians of the 20th century, as well as co-founder of the ACLU. She was the first deaf-blind person to earn a Bachelor of Arts degree. Helen campaigned for women's right to vote, labor rights, socialism, antimilitarism, and other similar causes. She was inducted into the Alabama Women's Hall of Fame and the Alabama Writers Hall of Fame. Helen proved to the world that deaf and blind people could all learn to communicate and are capable of doing things just like other people. She is an idol to many deaf and blind people in the world.

Early childhood and illness

Helen Adams Keller was born on June 27, 1880, in Tuscumbia, Alabama. She was a happy, healthy baby. Her father worked for a newspaper, while her mother was an educated woman who took care of her. At 19 months old, Helen contracted an unknown illness that left her both deaf and blind. After a period of time, she was able to communicate somewhat with Martha, the 6-year-old daughter of the family cook, who understood her signs. Gradually she learned to communicate with her family using signs. She also learned how to tell which person was walking by from the vibrations their footsteps would make. The sex and age of the person could be identified by how strong and continuous the steps were.

Helen further tried to understand her surroundings through touch, smell, and taste. However, she began to realize that her family members spoke to one another with their mouths instead of using signs as she did. Feeling their moving lips, she flew into a rage when she was unable to join in the conversation. By the age of six, "the need of some means of communication became so urgent that these outbursts occurred daily, sometimes hourly." She tormented Martha and inflicted raging tantrums on her parents. Many family relatives felt she should be institutionalized.

Education

Looking for answers and inspiration, in 1886, Helen's mother came across a travelogue in which the successful education of a deaf and blind girl was mentioned. This eventually led Helen to the Perkins Institute for the Blind in Boston, where it was suggested that she start working with Anne Sullivan. Anne herself had been visually impaired earlier and thus had a better understanding of Helen's condition. This was the beginning of a 49-year-long relationship during which Sullivan evolved into Helen's governess and eventually her companion.

Anne Sullivan arrived at Helen's house and began to teach her to communicate by spelling words into her hand. Helen was frustrated at first because she did not understand that every object had a word uniquely identifying it. As her frustration grew, so did her tantrums, but her teacher persisted with patience. Helen's big breakthrough in communication came the next month, when she realized that the motions her teacher was making on the palm of her hand, while running cool water over her other hand, symbolized the idea of "water". She then nearly exhausted her teacher demanding the names of all the other familiar objects in her world.

Starting in May 1888, Helen attended the Perkins Institute for the Blind, where a new world of friendship began: "I joined the little blind children in their work and play, and talked continually. I was delighted to find that nearly all of my new friends could spell with their fingers. Oh, what happiness! To talk freely with other children! To feel at home in the great world!"

In 1894, Helen moved to New York along with Anne Sullivan to learn from the school for the deaf. There, Helen worked on improving her communication skills and studied regular academic subjects. Impressed with her talent, drive, and determination, a sponsor agreed to pay for her college studies. In 1900, she gained admittance in Radcliffe College. She was accompanied by Sullivan, who sat by her side to interpret lectures and texts. By this time, Helen had mastered several methods of communication, including touch-lip reading, Braille, speech, typing, and finger-spelling. During these days, Helen wrote her first book *The Story of My Life* with the help of Sullivan and Sullivan's future husband, John Macy. At the age of 24, Keller graduated with honors to become the first deaf-blind person to earn a Bachelor of Arts degree. As she had rightly said, "When one door of happiness closes, another opens; but often we look so long at the closed door that we do not see the one which has been opened for us."

Lectures

Determined to communicate with others as conventionally as possible, besides sign language Helen had learned to speak with speech therapy and also to "hear" people's speech by reading their lips with her hands. Despite her disabilities, she had a strong inner voice, and hence started delivering speeches and lectures.

One of her lectures, which also appeared in a newspaper, reported: "Helen Keller spoke of the joy that life gave her. She was thankful for the faculties and abilities that she did possess and stated that the most productive pleasures she had were curiosity and imagination. Keller also spoke of the joy of service and the happiness that came from doing things for others... Keller imparted that 'helping your fellow men were one's only excuse for being in this world and in the doing of things to help one's fellows lay the secret of lasting happiness.' She also told of the joys of loving work and the happiness of achievement. The lecture had a profound impact on the audience."

Helen had an inspiring work ethic as well. She said, "I long to accomplish a great and noble task, but it is my chief duty to accomplish small tasks as if they were great and noble." Keller went on to become a world-famous speaker and author. She is remembered as an advocate for people with disabilities, amid numerous other causes. The deaf and blind community was widely impacted by her. In 1946, Helen was appointed counselor of international relations for the American Foundation of Overseas Blind. She traveled to 35 countries on five continents. At age 75, Helen embarked on the longest and most grueling trip of her life across Asia. Through her many speeches and appearances, she brought inspiration and encouragement to millions of people.

Political activities

Helen was a member of the Socialist Party and actively campaigned and wrote in support of the working class from 1909 to 1921. Many of her speeches and writings were about women's right to vote and the impacts of war. She was a radical socialist and also a birth control supporter. Although she faced opposition and criticism from some people, she continued with her work with determination.

Helen joined the Industrial Workers of the World in 1912. She was appointed on a commission to investigate the conditions of the blind. She wrote, "For the first time I, who had thought blindness a misfortune beyond human control, found that too much of it was traceable to wrong industrial conditions, often caused by the selfishness and greed of employers. And the social evil contributed its share. I found that poverty drove women to prostitution and syphilis, that ended in blindness."

In 1915, along with George Kessler, she founded the Helen Keller International (HKI) organization, which is devoted to research in vision, health, and nutrition. In 1920, she helped to found the American Civil Liberties Union (ACLU), which plays a major role in civil liberties cases to this day. She met every U.S. President from Grover Cleveland to Lyndon B. Johnson and was friends with many famous figures, including Alexander Graham Bell, Charlie Chaplin, and Mark Twain.

Writings

Helen wrote a total of 12 published books and several articles. At age 22, she published *The Story of My Life*, which recounts her life from childhood up to age 21. In 1908, she wrote *The World I Live In*, giving readers an insight into how she felt about the world. *Out of the Dark*, a series of essays on socialism, was published in 1913.

When Keller was young, she was introduced to Christianity. She said, "I always knew He was there, but I didn't know His name!" Her spiritual autobiography, *My Religion*, was published in 1927 and then in 1994 extensively revised and re-issued under the title *Light in My Darkness*. Keller described the progressive views of her belief in these words: "Since His Life cannot be less in one being than another, or His Love manifested less fully in one thing than another, His Providence must be universal . . . He has provided religion of some kind everywhere, and it does not matter to what race or creed anyone belongs if one is faithful to one's ideals of right living."

Later life

Helen suffered a series of strokes in 1961 and spent the last years of her life at her home. In 1964, President Johnson awarded her the Presidential Medal of Freedom, one of America's two highest civilian honors. In 1965 she was elected to the National Women's Hall of Fame. She devoted much of her later life to raising funds for the American Foundation for the Blind. She passed away in her sleep in 1968 at the age of 88.

Portrayals

Helen Keller's life has been interpreted several times in movies, documentaries, plays, and biographies. Her autobiography, *The Story of My Life*, was used as the basis for the 1957 television drama *The Miracle Worker*. The story was developed into a Broadway play in 1959 and an Oscar-winning feature film in 1962. The title echoes Mark Twain's description of Anne Sullivan as a "miracle worker." It describes the relationship between Helen and Anne, depicting how the teacher led her from a state of feral wildness into education, activism, and intellectual celebrity.

Posthumous honors

A preschool for the deaf and hard of hearing in Mysore, India, was originally named after Helen Keller. In 1999, Keller was listed in Gallup's Most Widely Admired People of the 20th century.

In 2003, Alabama honored its native daughter on its state quarter. The Helen Keller Hospital in Alabama is dedicated to her. Streets are named after Helen Keller in various countries. A stamp was issued in 1980 by the United States Postal Service depicting Keller and Sullivan, to mark the centennial of Keller's birth. In 2009, a bronze statue of Helen Keller was added to the National Statuary Hall Collection. The pedestal base bears a quotation in raised Latin and braille letters: "The best and most beautiful things in the world cannot be seen or even touched, they must be felt with the heart."

A beautiful line from an amazing personality, who demonstrated that there is no adversity and no darkness that can stop you from emerging into the light to lead a life of greatness.

● ● ●

Step 3

CAPABILITY

Whatever you become capable of manifests in your life.

A human being is the most beautiful creation of God. The irony is that this wonderful creation feels helpless on encountering failure! On facing failure, a person begins to consider one's life a waste and even forgets the very purpose of coming to Earth. The priceless life that you have received is not for wasting by getting caught up in the duality of success and failure; instead it is for always progressing ahead by converting every situation (even failure) into a ladder for growth. You may question, "How is it possible? We are happy on achieving success but dejected and depressed during failure." So, let us understand what will help you to convert failure into a ladder, and what will give you the confidence to tread the path of success with your head held high. It is CAPABILITY.

Human beings alone can think, understand, learn, and take decisions. By using these faculties, you can develop every aspect of your life and increase your capability. The right method to do so is to set new goals, identify the requirements to achieve those goals, and to build capabilities accordingly. This is the remedy for failure. The word 'capability' used in this chapter includes efficiency, capacity, eligibility, and aptitude. These help you to get prepared for attaining your goal.

Suppose a student has a dream of joining the army since childhood. He gets inspired whenever he sees any army men and tries to emulate their style standing in front of a mirror. As he grows up, he collects information about how fit he needs to be and the required physical and written tests to be taken for joining the army. Then according to those requirements, he works to build his capabilities. Thereafter he appears for the tests and successfully passes them in the first attempt.

This means if you can develop your capability according to your goal, then you can reach the pinnacle of success; provided you don't doubt your capacity. The first condition to achieve anything in life is that you should be capable for it. In other words, WHATEVER YOU BECOME CAPABLE OF MANIFESTS IN YOUR LIFE. Strong will power and lack of self-doubt accelerate this process of manifestation.

Now let's delve into the various factors that can help you to develop capability.

Prayer for enhancing your capability

Prayer is always the best start for everything. Capability can be increased by using the power of prayer. Prayer helps to make you receptive for the qualities that you wish to inculcate. There are many people around the globe who are able to execute the toughest tasks despite setbacks and failures, because they have prayed in the right way.

Relax your body and repeat a little word: "Help, Help, Help." Repeat it constantly. You can also sing it in a tune. The subconscious mind aligns faster with rhyme and rhythm. The most important element in a prayer is feeling. Thus, with a feeling of love and surrender, slowly pray in a rhythm filling in the blanks appropriately: "Help, Help, Help. Dear God, in order to achieve success in _____, please enhance the qualities of _____ within me. I will make all possible efforts that are required of me. Kindly help me and show me the path. Thank You very much."

Being in the present

Before developing any capability, you need to first develop the ability to live in the present. Most people keep brooding over past mistakes and are either lost in memories of the past or imaginations of the future. They lose focus over the present. Hence they cannot work with their full capacity and energy on their current activities. As a result, they are unable to develop their capabilities to the full.

You may have experienced that whenever your mind runs here and there, you cannot study or work as well as you could have. This means that unless you free yourself from the grip of the past or future, you would keep losing the present.

To do so, anchor your attention to the present while performing your daily tasks. The practice of meditation will help you in this. Meditate regularly. You can practice any meditation technique such as 'watching the breath', 'watching your thoughts', 'watching the sensations of the body', etc. to make the wavering mind dwell in the present.

Capability Mantra

Most often an ailment cannot be treated by a single dose. The dosage has to be consumed every day in small quantities until health is achieved. Likewise, if today you have set a goal for yourself, do not assume that you will become capable of achieving it the very same day. Competence and capability cannot be developed suddenly or in a hurry. For instance, a student who did not study the whole year, begins to study just a few days prior to the examinations—that too with the stress to achieve good grades, with his mind wandering in the past and future, and with regrets and thoughts that next year he will definitely study from the very beginning. Such a student can never gain the same competence as the student who studied a little bit every day throughout the year. So what happens to the student who procrastinated and is now trying to catch up? His mind will weave a yarn of excuses such as, "The syllabus is too much and too difficult... I cannot do it... I am not capable of doing this..." and so on.

This implies that we need to begin developing the capability much earlier and not right before the tests. No one can reach their goal without advanced preparation, be it a warrior like Emperor Shivaji or a leader like Mahatma Gandhi. Shivaji had to prepare himself for years to capture the forts back from the Mughals. He first learnt to run on rough terrain, climb hills and then smaller mountains with the help of ropes. He surely must have failed in his initial attempts. But this training made his body and arms strong enough due to which later on he could climb the biggest of mountains, scale the highest of walls, and jump from great heights. Only after rigorous combat training did he become capable of taking on the Mughals head-on.

Thus, the mantra for developing capability is: *A little but today*. This means do a little bit, but do it today. If you postpone it thinking you will do a lot tomorrow, then it may never happen. Hence, *a little but today*. By applying this mantra consistently, you will gradually become capable of achieving your goal. If a student cannot sit for two hours to study, let him sit for 15 minutes every day. Slowly he will become capable of sitting for two hours daily. If the mind says, "I am not capable enough," tell the mind, "Today it may seem that I am incapable, but I want to be capable and very soon I will be." If you are doing the right prayers and following the maxim *A little but today*, then you will definitely improve your capabilities.

Now let us look at some of the capabilities that need to be developed and how to develop them.

Capability of body, mind, and intellect

Do you find the tireless efforts of your body inspirational? If not, it's helpful to know that your body is working 24 hours a day, ever since the day you were born. Whether you are awake or in deep sleep, your body is always at your service.

To raise your physical capability, you need to first understand the constitution of your body. Is it lethargic, restless, or balanced? Observe yourself and identify at which time of the day your body is agile, when does it need more energy, when, how, and how much energy is spent throughout the day, when is your intellectual capacity used the most, and so on. Physical capability can be enhanced with balanced diet, exercise, work, and rest. Only a physically capable body can help you develop other capabilities.

On the other hand, a physically capable body cannot work at its best unless the mind and intellect too are trained. If the mind is habituated to running here and there and the intellect is too lazy to contemplate about anything, your overall capability cannot improve. Capabilities of the mind and intellect can be enhanced by meditation and deep contemplation. Contemplation helps you go deep into any subject. You become proficient in understanding every aspect of that subject at a minute level. Contemplation helps to take correct decisions. Through the mind, body, and intellect's capable functioning and efficiency, new doors to success will open and any failure can be overcome.

One more essential training for your mind to develop capability is: to learn to celebrate other people's joy. If others' success makes you unhappy, it indicates that you have not become capable of being successful. Do not let your mind be the breeding ground of jealousy, comparison, hatred, and despair. Instead of feeling despondent at others' success, it's a good idea to make some more efforts for your own success and enhance your capability. A great attitude in this situation would be: "If others can win, so can I." As you become more and more capable in your work, the closer success gets to you. There will come a time when no one, including yourself, will be able to stop you from reaching the pinnacle of success. You will also begin to understand the secret of others' success in detail.

In addition to your conscious mind, you also need to train your subconscious mind for cultivating capability. Your subconscious mind considers any thought that you keep on repeating as true. Then it presents evidences to you corresponding with that thought, which in turn converts that thought into a firm belief. When you constantly think, "I am not capable of doing this… it is impossible for me to do this… I can never take the right decisions…" etc., your subconscious mind considers these thoughts to be true. Then whenever some incidents take place, your subconscious mind makes you react to those incidents in accordance with these thoughts. And then you say, "Didn't I tell you? It is impossible for me to do this…"

If you want to raise your capabilities, you need to change the programming of your subconscious mind. Re-program it with voice of faith. Instead of saying, "I cannot do this job," say, "Until now I was unable to do this job, but now I will be able to do it because I have received knowledge and guidance. This will definitely help me to accomplish this job with full capability. I am bound to succeed. Nothing is impossible for me. Success is my nature." Repeat many such statements that strengthen your belief.

Lie down, relax, and repeat certain statements to re-program your subconscious mind. For example, say to yourself, "I am becoming capable with love, joy, and peace." Say this again and again with faith so that it re-programs your subconscious. The more rhythmically and lovingly you say it, the better. Start doing this every day and the important thing is to avoid checking constantly whether the desired result is occurring or not. One day you will suddenly feel the difference in your thinking and you will be surprised. As we have seen, this is a very good method to break wrong thinking patterns and a great remedy for overcoming failure.

Identify and accept your limitations

You are the Supreme Consciousness or the Universal Self. You are limitless, but your vehicle, i.e. your physical body, may have some limitations despite breaking free from your comfort zone. Even an expert driver cannot run an 800cc car at the same speed as that of a sports car. A driver's proficiency lies in understanding the capacity of his vehicle including its weaknesses, strengths, and limitations, and then driving it with 100% efficiency according to its maximum capacity.

What is being said is, do not copy others' goals. Set a goal according to the nature and disposition of your body-mind and develop your capability with that goal in mind. Someone might not have the innate sense of music but may write well. He cannot become a great singer, no matter how much he tries. But if he works on his skill in the field of writing, then he can surely become a good writer.

Do not undertake something just because a neighbor or a friend is doing it or because it is associated with more money and glamour. Choose work that aligns with your nature, because only then you can remain happy. And a happy person never fails.

Capability to make right decisions

In spite of possessing the capability, some people do not become as successful as they could have, owing to the lack of decision making skills. They are unable to take the right decision at the right time. Decision making skill involves the ability to declare: "It is my decision and I take full responsibility for it, irrespective of whether the results are positive or negative. I will neither take credit for its success nor will I blame others for its failure." Thus, one needs to be capable enough to take responsibility of decision making.

Often people do not want to take the responsibility of decision making as they are afraid, "What if my decision is wrong…" They cannot bear to be blamed. They want others to take even their personal decisions so that if the decision turns out to be wrong, they can have someone else to blame. Such people depend on others for every small decision.

The art of decision making can be learnt only by making decisions. If a decision turns out to be wrong, you should try to diminish its negative consequences. In this way, accept the consequences of your decisions. Acceptance will mitigate the negative thoughts and the guilt associated with the wrong decision. Even wrong decisions help you to evolve because they too teach a lot of important lessons.

Hence everyone should learn to take their own decisions and also take responsibility of its results. Only then can they progress in life.

Capability to maintain and honor relationships

In modern times, man has become too self-centered. People find most relationships a burden and stick to only those relations that might prove beneficial. Even those relations begin to feel redundant after the value quotient is lost. Most people believe that relationships pose a hurdle to their progress. The truth is actually the opposite. Relationships are in fact the most helpful factors in our growth. As we build the capability of maintaining and honoring relationships, several virtues develop within us in the process. These virtues include unconditional love, compassion, selflessness, humility, patience, quality of giving, forgiveness, giving a thought to others, communication, and most importantly bowing down or letting go of ego.

Our ego is hurt if we have to bow in a relationship when we have made some mistake and sometimes even when we haven't. The ego does not wish to bend. It is relationships that help you to glimpse your ego. The ego surrenders only if you work on it with understanding. If the ego learns to surrender, then your progress is tremendous, both in worldly life as well as on the spiritual path. Therefore observe carefully which quality each relationship is cultivating within you.

Understanding the role of every relationship, give importance to each of them. Build the capability within you of making all your relationships better and healthier. Reading books and receiving guidance from your spiritual master or your elders will help you in this process.

Also, observe people who share good relationships with others and try to comprehend their qualities and their understanding of relationships. Such earnest efforts will create ways to make your relationships harmonious and warm. This will help you to overcome failures in your personal as well as professional fields.

Meditation for raising your capability

Let us now proceed to an exercise called *Believe Meditation*. This meditation will help to raise your capability. First read the entire meditation given below, internalize it or record it, and then practice this meditation every day for maximum benefit.

1. Sit in a chosen posture with a particular *mudra* (positioning of the fingers) and close your eyes. Gently tell yourself the following...
2. I BELIEVE — that developing capability begins with faith.
3. I BELIEVE — that physical deficiencies and lack of material

comfort are illusory realities. These do not determine whether I am a failure or a success. And despite these factors, I can augment my capabilities.

4. I BELIEVE — that sarcastic remarks of relatives, taunts of friends, and clashes with boss or colleagues are nothing but words uttered in unconsciousness and ignorance. Hence they do not affect me at all.

5. I BELIEVE — that I am the unlimited and powerful Self. I am eternal... I am what I have always been... I existed before this body... I existed before this name... I existed before this work... I existed before these friends... I existed before this role. Having experienced this, I know that my body-mind, which is the vehicle of the Self, is capable of combating any failures and cultivating the qualities needed for supreme success.

6. I BELIEVE — that the one who existed before everything is the most important. In the presence of the eternal I, everything gets done happily and successfully.

7. I BELIEVE — that the problems I was facing a few moments ago are not occurring *with* me, they are *for* me, so that I can learn to face them and grow.

8. I BELIEVE — that my body is a miraculous instrument and by training it I can gain other capabilities.

9. I BELIEVE — that acceptance is the first step towards success. I accept the limitations of my body-mind and proceed towards success in spite of them.

10. I BELIEVE — that all my decisions should arise from my true eternal self, from the understanding of truth, in accordance with higher teachings, and knowing all the facts.

11. I BELIEVE — that I have always been free and will always be

free. Any negativity in my life is not a failure but a necessity for training my body-mind.

12. I BELIEVE — that my body-mind is a vessel for the Self to express itself as love, bliss, stillness, courage, and creativity.
13. I BELIEVE — that there is a state of unshakable faith, which is attained on realizing my true self — Self Realization. No doubts remain thereafter.
14. I BELIEVE — that no matter what kind of body I have, it is capable of realizing the Self. That is true success.
15. Now slowly open your eyes and with complete belief and faith start fulfilling your dreams.

SUMMARY:

1. What will help you to convert failure into a ladder and what will give you the confidence to tread the path of success with your head held high is CAPABILITY.
2. The first condition to achieve anything in life is that you should be capable for it. In other words, *whatever you become capable of manifests in your life*. Strong will power and lack of self-doubt accelerate this process of manifestation.
3. Capability can be increased by using the power of prayer. Prayer helps to make you receptive for the qualities that you wish to inculcate.
4. Anchor your attention to the present while performing your daily tasks. Practicing meditation will help in anchoring your mind in the present.
5. The mantra for developing capability is: *A little but today.*
6. Physical capability can be enhanced with balanced diet, exercise, work, and rest. Capabilities of the mind and intellect

can be enhanced by meditation and deep contemplation. Subconscious mind can be reprogrammed with voice of faith.

7. One more essential training for your mind to develop capability is: to learn to celebrate other people's joy.
8. Do not copy others' goals. Set a goal according to the nature and disposition of your body-mind and develop your capability with that goal in mind.
9. Learn to take your own decisions and also take responsibility of its results. Only then can you progress in life.
10. As you build the capability of maintaining and honoring relationships, several virtues develop within you in the process.

***

"Striving for success without hard work
is like trying to harvest where you haven't planted."

— David Bly

FORGIVENESS PRAYER

Dear God, please forgive me
for harboring thoughts and fears of failure.
Please forgive everyone who contributed to my failure, including me.
I am sorry for any feelings of guilt, sorrow, anger, or vengeance.
Kindly forgive and heal all the causes and consequences of failure.
Forgive me for considering this situation as a failure.
I am sorry for believing myself a failure.
I forgot I am a part of God, so what's true for God is true for me.
If God cannot fail, how can I?
Recognizing my divine nature,
I proclaim that I am in favor of success and not failure.
I claim complete success and I am achieving it.
Thank You... Thank You... Thank You.

STEP 4

LEARNING

*Cultivating the art of learning
is like receiving the master key of success in your hand.*

Knowledge is power. Knowledge can take you to the peak of success. Knowledge is gained by learning. Hence learning is a major factor to avoid or overcome failure. So, let's tee off and unravel the secret of learning. Reading this book is the first step in this direction.

Learning the art of learning

'Art of learning' is a quality that automatically keeps you away from unnecessary actions like back biting, complaining, blaming, unhealthy competition, and the like. Your focus would be only on learning and thereby everything else takes a backseat. Thus, this quality not only helps in raising your capability but also protects you from other demerits. In fact, cultivating the art of learning is like receiving the master key of success in your hand.

Let us take an example of cooking, which can then be applied to any other field.

In most families in India, girls are taught to cook a variety of dishes, so that they can cook well for their new family after marriage.

However, this training may not prove to be useful if they are not taught the art of learning. Suppose a girl knows how to cook brinjal curry but her new family prefers cottage cheese curry. She has been taught several dishes but not how to learn, which leads to problems.

If your girl knows how to learn, then in her new family she will observe and soon pick up how to cook the dishes of their liking. Thus, instead of many dishes, it's better to teach your daughter the art of learning—how to observe and cook a similar dish, how to enhance one's observation power, how to use common sense during cooking, what are the basic principles of cooking, as well as how to innovate. She should be able to watch and understand what others do differently due to which their food is delicious and healthy. Subtle observation helps one to become an expert. Also, teach your child how to observe others' virtues and imbibe them.

The essence of this example is applicable to any area of life.

Field-related Learning

Complete knowledge related to any field is essential to scale the height of success in that particular field. One should know about all the positive and negative aspects of that field. If one is facing failure, it indicates that knowledge is lacking in some aspect. Hence, put in all your efforts to learn everything you can about your chosen field.

Learning from mistakes

On encountering failure, one often blames others. Full credit of success is taken by oneself while the blame for failure is heaped on others. For instance, "I failed because my teacher did not teach well; I did not get a job due to partiality by the management; I didn't get a promotion because I never indulged in appeasing my boss; I could not go for higher studies due to my parents' narrow-minded thinking; I did not get a good life partner, otherwise I would have attained such great success…"

We are unable to reflect upon our mistakes and the causes of our failures due to the tendency of blaming others. As a result, we don't think upon what should be done to succeed and put a full stop to the topic. There is no question of learning with this attitude. But once we are free from the habit of blaming others, we pave the way for positive occurrences in our life. This is because the mind is freed of negative feelings like fear, anger, and hatred as soon as it stops blaming others. We are able to stay calm and focus on the task at hand instead of finding faults in others. We are able to learn from our mistakes and take the right steps to rectify them. Consequently, success comes knocking at our door.

Learning by observation

We learn a lot by observing the world around. We get molded according to our surrounding environment and people. Our language, behavior, and belief systems become just like the people around us.

Therefore, the company of experts in your chosen field will help you immensely in developing the qualities required in that field. That is why medical students work as assistants with experienced doctors after completing their studies. Similarly, in other fields too, people work under veterans of that field to hone their skills and abilities.

Thus, whichever topic, field, or qualities you wish to gain proficiency in, try to seek the company of those people who are experts in those aspects. Observe them, read their autobiographies, and listen to their experiences.

In order to learn by observing, your observation power needs to be acute. The best example is Eklavya who would observe Master

Dronacharya teaching archery to Arjuna. Eklavya's observation power was so acute that one day he became a better archer than Arjuna.

People with piercing observation and higher receptivity are able to learn even from those things that go unnoticed by others. Lord Dattatreya learnt life lessons from 24 living as well as non-living elements of nature, and considered them as his teachers.

Learning from our mirror

In nature's classroom there are no specific teachers assigned. People around us are our teachers—if we learn the art of learning. Nature teaches us through the people around us. Some people teach us through their positivity and others through their negativity. Our attitude should be of learning, irrespective of the kind of people. This is one of the main steps to combat failure. To understand this step, two points are to be kept in mind:

1. The world is our mirror. All the people in our life are our reflection.
2. The fault lies not in the other person but in the eye of the beholder, in the false beliefs of the beholder.

We feel good in the presence of some people, while some people's presence makes us feel awful. It is not their fault. They are merely reflecting our state of mind. Whatever faults we perceive in other people or out in the world, those faults exist within us, and that is why they are visible to us in the mirror of our world. The correction needs to made within us. Once the faults are corrected within, the mirror will reflect the same. At the same time, we should contemplate what false beliefs we harbor due to which we feel that the world or other people are wrong. In this way, we would be learning at the highest level.

Learning about people

There are various types of people in the world. We need the support of people to achieve success. But without studying and understanding people, we cannot gain their support. Depending on their nature and behavior, people can be divided into 7 categories. We need to understand these categories and also identify to which one we belong. Our goal should be to belong to the seventh one.

For a lighter touch, let's understand the 7 categories using the metaphor of fruits and vegetables.

1. *Bitter Gourd people.* As the name suggests these are bitter people who perpetuate crime. They spread terror and unrest in society.

2. *Mango people* (*aam insaan* in Hindi) or the common man. They are not involved in crime, but they live a mechanical, routine life. They simply do what others do, as if leading an unconscious life. They merely imitate others' lifestyles. They do not have their own thinking or opinion. *Mango people* are emotionally weak. As soon as someone praises them, they fall for it. There are some people who try to get something from others by using flattery, for instance, getting a treat or a party, or getting some work done by coworkers, and so on. Mango people easily fall for such tricks. They need to be trained to be careful while dealing with such manipulative people.

3. *Walnut People.* Inside the shell, a walnut looks just like a human brain. Thus, people of this category are those who make use of their intellect. They have learnt to make decisions by applying logic and reason. When people rise above being the 'common man,' their brain begins to work towards achieving success.

4. *Apple People.* They are like Newton who saw an apple falling and discovered gravity. People of this category use both their heads and their hearts.

5. *Lemon Orange Juice People.* After the activation of head and heart, some people move towards lemon and some towards orange. Lemons have generally been associated with rituals and *tantra* in religious context. Thus, some people choose the path of *tantra* due to their attraction towards *siddhis* or spiritual powers. The color orange or ochre has been associated with spiritual knowledge. Thus, some people attain spiritual knowledge and consider themselves to be 'wise'. Hence the risk at this stage is that some people move towards lemon and some towards orange. However, the true destination of every human being is the juice, i.e. from form to formlessness. The outer rind dissolves, the form is lost and what remains is the 'juice'—the essence, the Consciousness, the formless and limitless Self. That's the ultimate goal of every individual.

6. *Sprout People.* These are the people in whom the Consciousness has begun to sprout or germinate. These people begin to experience Self realization, yet they are not completely risk free. Since the sprouts or shoots are still tender, these people can easily get attracted to something and stray away from the path of truth. Spiritual powers may attract them. Thus, they have attained Self realization but the desire for name and fame may arise and lead them astray.

7. The seventh category of people is those who are permanently established in the experience of Self, i.e. Self stabilization. They are in no danger of falling off the path of truth. They are *risk free*. They have no danger from their internal ego or external events. Not even a storm can shake them. They have become like a supreme magnet that attracts only the best and the highest.

True learning

From the above categorization we realize that *actual learning is knowledge of your true self, and true success is getting stabilized in your true self.* Therefore, your goal should be to become the seventh type of truly successful person—a supreme magnet, where the individual ego melts and you become Consciousness. ('Individual ego' means the sense of separateness from the rest of Creation). By following the path of learning, you have to become free and risk free. Free from individual ego and risk free from any factors that can shake your mind. You need to find and annihilate every possibility that can enslave your mind to the worldly illusion. For this you will have to observe yourself in various events that occur in your life and identify the risk factors that still exist within you.

Learning about yourself

Now that we know all seven types of people, which category do you think you fit in: Apple or Mango, Bitter Gourd, or Walnut? If you are reading this, then you are certainly not Bitter Gourd, and you have definitely transcended the Mango category. But you should be aware of the risk in the fifth category (Lemon Orange Juice). You should strive for the juice and not Orange or Lemon.

If your consciousness has sprouted, then watch out for those aspects in your environment that can damage or harm this tender sprout. Contemplate on what should be done to protect yourself from those risk factors.

Observe that throughout the day what kind of incidents you encounter in which the negativities (illusory realities) weigh you down and make you feel depressed? Let's understand with an example. Suppose a person wants to park his car and he sees a board: 'Parking for two-wheelers only.' Seeing that board, he removes two wheels from his car; only to realize that further down there is a parking bay available for cars too! This is a joke but many a time this is how we believe in illusory reality and act accordingly. Therefore, make a list of all those areas in which illusory realities overwhelm you, recognize them as illusory reality, and start dealing with them with the new understanding that you have gained in this book.

Once you find your Achilles heel, then with the right knowledge resort to the right prayer, and soon your weak areas will subside.

The quality of being risk free is the infallible weapon against failure. For this you have to discipline your mind and body. This is the preparation for Self stabilization, as this body will become the medium for Self expression. Else you will have to bear the tantrums of the body. This however does not mean you have to neglect your body. If your body is suffering from an illness, give it adequate rest and also take it to a doctor. However, pampering the body needs to be avoided. With foresight, start cultivating good habits and begin with baby steps right now. Our body-mind listens to us. If we tell it that it *has to* work for a particular time, it will obey. Thus, on attaining the right understanding, you will easily be able to train your body and not waste any spare time.

To test and identify your level of consciousness, you have to understand what attracts you. Attraction from below signifies worldly desires and attraction from above indicates desire for Self Stabilization and Expression (true success). So what attracts you— the lower desires or the higher Self? The list below signifies the attributes that indicate a higher pull and thereby it can be considered as an action plan to move higher.

You are attracted to higher levels if…

Physical level – For making your body clean and pure like a temple, you are cultivating good food habits, have reduced or stopped overly spicy or sweet foods, and exercise regularly.

Mental Level – Your focus, concentration, and inner peace is increasing.

Social level – You are increasingly becoming free of hatred, anger, stress, unconsciousness, boredom, lethargy, and backbiting; if you focus on people's virtues instead of their flaws, and if your relationships are becoming warmer with everyone.

Financial Level – You spend wisely because you have understood the difference between 'need' and 'want'. Your attraction towards material things has reduced and you no longer experience shortage of money. The goal of your life has totally changed since you have understood the profound secret that money is the means and not the destination.

Spiritual Level – You are not getting stuck in events occurring in your life, you meditate once or twice a day, you contemplate on higher teachings, you are opening up and blossoming, your happiness level is rising, you are able to stay on Self more and more.

SUMMARY:

1. Knowledge can take you to the peak of success. Knowledge is gained by learning. Hence learning is a major factor to avoid or overcome failure.

2. Complete knowledge related to any field is essential to scale the height of success in that field. If one is facing failure, it indicates that knowledge is lacking in some aspect.

3. Nature teaches us through the people around us. Some people teach us through their positivity and others through their negativity.
4. Cultivating the art of learning is like receiving the master key of success in your hand.
5. Whichever topic, field, or qualities you wish to gain proficiency in, try to seek the company of those people who are experts in those aspects.
6. Nature gives us clues and indications; we should learn to identify and understand them, and take actions accordingly.
7. We need the support of people to achieve success. Hence we need to understand the 7 categories of people.
8. Actual learning is knowledge of your true self, and true success is getting stabilized in your true self.
9. By following the path of learning, you have to become free and risk free. Free from individual ego and risk free from any factors that can shake your mind.
10. The quality of being risk free is the infallible weapon against failure. For this the body and mind needs to be disciplined. What attracts you—the lower desires or the higher Self?

* * *

Luminous Lives

OPRAH WINFREY

*"I don't believe in failure.
It is not failure if you enjoyed the process."*
— Oprah Winfrey

The desire to accomplish something despite encountering failures makes one execute extraordinary feats. One is able to maintain the passion to cross every hurdle, be it financial, familial, or societal. One is consumed with just one yearning: fulfillment of one's goal. And the desire to learn something makes it possible to set a powerful goal. Oprah Winfrey is a living example of this.

Early life

Oprah was born into poverty to an unmarried teen mother, *Vernita Lee,* in a farm in Mississippi on January 29, 1954. Her father *Vernon Winfrey* was in the armed forces. Soon after her birth, her unmarried parents separated. Oprah was then raised by her grandmother, Hatti Mae Lee, in rural poverty. At the age of six, she returned to her mother who could not give her time or attention because of her work as a housemaid. Oprah resorted to various antics to gain attention of her mother such as stealing, breaking a glass, or faking memory loss, but often found herself alone. Being alone at home, she claims she was molested repeatedly by male relatives and a family friend. She became a rebellious, troubled adolescent. At the age of 14, Oprah's mother sent her to live with her father in Nashville, Tennessee. Oprah's father was very strict but encouraging and made education the number one priority for her.

Despite being deprived of parental love, she did not feel dejected or inferior. She did not allow her past to determine her future. She demonstrated that regardless of the obstacles we face, we can achieve anything through learning, passion, determination, and hard work. She grew to be very good in studies and a favorite of teachers. As a result, she received the award for the most popular girl in school. She was ever keen to learn. She won various debate competitions and also the crown of Miss Black Tennessee beauty pageant.

Television Star

A person's inclination is evident in childhood itself. Oprah would interview her dolls while other children played with toys. Her high school friend Anthony Otey says that Oprah was focused on the future and her goals. She always endeavored to meet her goals and today she has fulfilled her dreams.

Oprah won a scholarship to Tennessee State University where she majored in Speech Communications and Performing Arts. While rehearsing for a drama in high school, she was spotted by a local radio station and given the opportunity to become a news reader. She had to struggle a lot in the beginning owing to her African-American origin. She was told her looks were unfit for television because her "hair's too thick, nose is too wide, and chin's too big." She did not let this keep her down for long. She dusted herself and moved ahead to become a television anchor in another city. She did not let her so-called bad looks come in the way of her success. She says, "I don't think of myself as a poor deprived ghetto girl who made good. I think of *myself* as somebody who from an early age knew I was responsible for myself and I had to make good."

It is this belief that made her successful from the beginning of her career. She was the youngest and the first African-American woman to be given the honor to be a news anchor in WLS TV. Thereafter, there was no looking back.

In 1983, Oprah went to Chicago to host WLS TV's talk show *A.M. Chicago*. It had very low ratings and Oprah made some changes. The first episode of this show was aired on January 2, 1994, which was not very successful. But within months, her magic worked, and the show went from last place to becoming the highest rated talk show in Chicago. It was renamed as *The Oprah Winfrey Show* and started broadcasting on national television. It won 3 Emmy Awards for two consecutive years. In 1988, she was honored with *The Broadcaster Of The Year* award by the International Radio and Television Society. She was the youngest person and only the fifth woman ever to receive the honor. She has become a television icon. She says, "Be thankful for what you have; you'll end up having more. If you concentrate on what you don't have, you will never ever have enough."

Oprah on the silver screen

Oprah made her debut in the film industry with Steven Spielberg's movie *The Color Purple* in 1985. She played the role of a confident and daring woman and proved that she was a capable actor. She was nominated for the Academy Award for the Best Supporting Role. Next year, in 1986, she established her own production company *Harpo Studios* which demonstrated her love for the film industry.

Her agony

Apart from her professional life, when we look at Oprah's personal life, especially her early years, it raises her to even higher levels. Oprah, who has brought light to so many people's life, had to face a life filled with darkness and difficulties throughout her childhood and youth. She always had to fight for love. She was deprived of her parents' love in childhood and her dreams for a loving partner were shattered many a time in her youth. She faced sexual abuse in childhood. Poverty was rubbed in her face by other students in her school. She suffered from racial abuse too. However, she said, 'I'm black, I don't feel burdened by it and I don't think it's a huge responsibility. It's part of who I am. It does not define me." She had all the reasons that could push any other person into the bottomless pits of failure and dejection. But she did not give in because she believed wounds should be turned into wisdom.

Social work

Because of everything she had faced in her early life, Oprah could have blamed and retaliated against society after becoming rich and famous. However, she turned to social work. In 1991, she started a campaign to create a national database of convicted child abusers, and in 1993 President Bill Clinton signed the 'Oprah bill' into law. Oprah's movement was successful. In 1998, she formed a charity called as *Angel Network* which was involved in various projects such as providing education supplies, school construction, disaster relief, etc. In 2007, she established the *Oprah Winfrey Leadership Academy for Girls* in South Africa to provide world-class education to girls belonging to poor families. She considers her students as her daughters. She has donated millions of dollars for various causes and is considered "the greatest Black philanthropist in American history." In an interview Oprah said that she has reached that stage of life where she is free to do everything that she had dreamt of.

Even today she is enthusiastic about life and always willing to learn. She says, "I don't believe in failure. It is not failure if you enjoyed the process" and "Failure is just life trying to move us in another direction."

Success begins with you

Oprah has proved herself a complete artist by wearing the many hats of an anchor, a media proprietor, an actor, a producer, and a writer. She is considered "the richest African American of the 20th century" and "the world's most influential woman of her generation." She has been honored with numerous prestigious awards from around the world. However, what is unprecedented and unparalleled is the close relationship she has established with her admirers globally with her noble heart. She sums her story of success in her belief that *you* are responsible for your life and in order to be successful it is not important what your background is; success begins with you.

●●●

Step 5

QUALITIES

*Patience and consistency are essential
for developing qualities required to attain success.*

Developing good qualities, skills, and proficiency is crucial to befriend success. Success and qualities go hand in hand. Hence always focus on enhancing your qualities. Some of the main qualities needed for success are fearlessness, capability, completing jobs successfully, feeling of abundance, acceptance, taking responsibility, ease in every activity, amiability, unbreakable faith, benevolence, firmness, foresightedness, courage, self-respect, honesty, total growth, inspiration, lots of energy, *viveka* or ability to discriminate between real and unreal, efficiency, creativity, listening to your heart, etc. You may wonder how can these qualities be cultivated and whether you can master so many. The answer is YES. You can. Some important factors are given below that will help to develop these qualities.

Laws of Thought

There are 7 Universal Laws of Thought[*]. One of the most important law is the Law of Focus. According to this law:

---

[*] You can read about all the laws in the bestseller book *The Source* by Sirshree.

Success begins with you

Oprah has proved herself a complete artist by wearing the many hats of an anchor, a media proprietor, an actor, a producer, and a writer. She is considered "the richest African American of the 20th century" and "the world's most influential woman of her generation." She has been honored with numerous prestigious awards from around the world. However, what is unprecedented and unparalleled is the close relationship she has established with her admirers globally with her noble heart. She sums her story of success in her belief that *you* are responsible for your life and in order to be successful it is not important what your background is; success begins with you.

•••

STEP 5

QUALITIES

*Patience and consistency are essential
for developing qualities required to attain success.*

Developing good qualities, skills, and proficiency is crucial to befriend success. Success and qualities go hand in hand. Hence always focus on enhancing your qualities. Some of the main qualities needed for success are fearlessness, capability, completing jobs successfully, feeling of abundance, acceptance, taking responsibility, ease in every activity, amiability, unbreakable faith, benevolence, firmness, foresightedness, courage, self-respect, honesty, total growth, inspiration, lots of energy, *viveka* or ability to discriminate between real and unreal, efficiency, creativity, listening to your heart, etc. You may wonder how can these qualities be cultivated and whether you can master so many. The answer is YES. You can. Some important factors are given below that will help to develop these qualities.

Laws of Thought

There are 7 Universal Laws of Thought[*]. One of the most important law is the Law of Focus. According to this law:

---

[*] You can read about all the laws in the bestseller book *The Source* by Sirshree.

What you focus on, increases. This means that whatever you focus your attention on, it grows and manifests within you. Within every human being exists an amazing power: the power to focus one's attention. Any quality can be imbibed by using this power. Therefore always remember to focus on the good qualities of people, not their flaws. Many a time we enjoy criticizing others by highlighting their deficiencies and indirectly try to prove our own superiority. Unfortunately, in this process, the same flaws start developing within us. Hence the need to avoid this.

Secondly, we need to consciously focus on the virtues of people, not on their position in their company or in society. Furthermore, whatever position we may attain professionally or socially, our focus should be on developing our qualities. We should not be led astray by the praises of people and start focusing only on name, fame, and wealth. Developing divine qualities and attaining final success should be our goal.

It is also important to remember that if we focus on various things, then the power of our attention gets divided. Focused attention can create miracles. Therefore always keep your focus on the one whom you consider your ideal. This will activate the development of all the virtues within you that your ideal has.

Patience

It is said that good things come to those who wait. When you hear the word 'patience,' you may assume that all you have to do is set your intention, then sit around twiddling your thumbs, and wait for good things to come flooding in. That's not the case. But, you also don't have to struggle and suffer in order to achieve what you want.

The words 'action' and 'reaction' appear more attractive to people than 'patience'. We are so used to *doing* that we find it difficult to simply *be*—because we are conditioned to believe that always doing something is better, and that it's the only way to achieve anything.

But patience is not a passive trait. It is a powerful dynamic state that can take you through every adversity and guarantee your success.

Suppose you are trying to break a big rock with a hammer. Although you are striking hard repeatedly, the rock doesn't break. You might strike and a chip breaks away but you see little progress. You keep at it nonetheless. Eventually, when you land the hundredth strike, the rock breaks. So, were the earlier 99 strikes in vain? No. Those strikes had weakened the stone. The 99 strikes were, in fact, the strikes of patience. All the successful people in the world possess this quality, be it Edison, Nelson Mandela, J. K. Rowling, and others. Patience is a must to achieve success—be it success in achieving your goal or in developing qualities. This is because cultivating qualities required for your goal takes time and effort. Hence the need for patience.

Most people feel that the period during which they have to keep patience is very boring. This is because they are not aware of the wonder that is set into motion when we abide in the stillness of patience. By patiently allowing things to unfold, you have a golden opportunity to be in the moment, to enjoy the process, to marvel at the miraculous ways things come together, to learn, and to experience your *being*. Patience gives you the opportunity to experience happiness in both, the process and the result. With contemplation and patience, you can unwrap the hidden gifts, solutions, and life lessons from any situation, setback, or failure.

There are some things that may require extreme patience. If you sow a seed of black bamboo, you have to patiently tend to it for several months before the seed even sprouts. But once it sprouts, it grows to the height of 30 feet within three months! This is the fruit of patience. So, whenever you have to exhibit great patience, remember the black bamboo example: wait long enough, and you will get astonishingly fast results as reward for your patience. Patience is never in vain. All you have to do is continue taking inspired action patiently with persistence.

If your goal is small, patience doesn't matter; you can achieve that goal even by working impatiently. However, if your goal is grand, then you must be patient and persistent until you achieve it. Patience will help you in every aspect of life. It will prevent problems that can lead to failures and setbacks in various areas of life. And if you are facing failure, then patience will help you get back on track on the path of success.

In today's 'instant era,' we want to acquire everything '*a.s.a.p.*' (as soon as possible). We want to complete many tasks in a short time, we want to develop good qualities instantly, we want to achieve success instantly. We have become accustomed to impatience and immediate gratification. This often leads to disappointment. We are not happy when we have to wait, but there are many things that just cannot manifest instantly in our lives. Not everything we wish for happens a.s.a.p. Rather they happen in perfect order at the perfect time by 'A.S.P.' (Abiding in the Self with Patience). We need to prepare patiently and wait consciously, to allow the universe to synchronize harmoniously.

Suppose you are waiting to manifest a new car, you can perhaps take time to learn to drive, learn about the new car, or clean out your parking space to make room for it. In other words, while waiting for things to manifest in life, prepare the space within you to be able to receive it when it arrives. When you raise your receptivity for something, forces are set into motion in the unseen that make it happen.

The magical power of patience can be summed up as: WATCH, WAIT with WONDER! The three words, Watch, Wait and Wonder, possess extraordinary power. They help anchor you in the present moment and prevent you from constantly swinging between past and future. You will get an idea of the power of these words only when you start applying them to your life.

For most people, waiting is agonizing. They cannot stop thinking about the future. They not only miss out on the joy of the moment, but also often ruin things in the state of restlessness by trying to force things to evolve too quickly. With the help of 'Watch, Wait with Wonder' you witness wonders happening during the waiting period.

Most people give the right responses at the wrong time or the wrong responses at the right time. This complicates their life situations—personal and professional. As people do not know when and how much to wait, the problem that was about to be resolved, remains unsolved.

For example, if you are having an argument with your spouse, you may be choosing the wrong responses or the wrong timing due to lack of patience. You may lose your temper and start yelling. You don't have to do this. If you learn the art of waiting and responding at the right time, the argument won't escalate. You may be tempted to respond impulsively to your spouse's seemingly unacceptable words and try to get back at him or her. Just restrain yourself… be patient… and respond when you have your emotions under control. Your words and actions will then be based on love and not on hate.

Learning the art of waiting transforms a reactive way of life into a creative experience.

Develop the ability to take a step back and witness everything. Be aware of your physical reactions, your impulses, emotions, and thoughts. If you simply observe how something is making you feel, and give it just a few moments before responding, you will begin to grasp the art of 'responding' rather than 'reacting.'

When a music composer creates a piece of music, he introduces pauses between the notes. He intuitively senses how long to wait before playing the next note. The pauses between each note lend depth to the music. His intuitive waiting brings beauty and harmony to the composition.

Similarly, when we become experts at waiting for the right period of time and taking action at the right time, life falls into a beautiful rhythm and is attuned with the highest vibration of the universe.

Meditation is a practice that teaches patience. The experience of *being* that deepens with the practice of meditation lends wonder, bliss, and contentment to every moment of life. The body can be trained to remain still. The mind can be trained to remain focused. Meditation teaches us the art of waiting. Waiting gives us the laser focus necessary to give the correct commands to the universe.

Consistency

We have already seen that if a hundred blows of a hammer are required to break a rock, it doesn't mean that only the hundredth blow was successful. The first 99 blows were as important as the last. If someone stops working because it seems as though nothing is happening after the first few strikes, it means he is not aware of the next main quality needed for success: Consistency. Along with patience, consistency is essential.

One may ask why consistency is always emphasized so much. This is so because, firstly, the nature of certain goals is that a particular number of steps are required to reach it. Not giving up and working on it consistently are the only sure-fire methods to ensure your success. Like in the example of the rock, what needs to be clearly understood is that the first 99 blows were not "failures" but the steps towards the goal. Secondly, consistency is the fundamental quality that helps you to develop other qualities or skills. Without consistency, you cannot develop skills or reach the peak of success. Hence it is rightly said: *Consistency is the key to success.*

The highest possibility exists in every person and object, and it needs to manifest. Consistency plays a primary role in manifesting this possibility. The one who exercises every day or at least thrice a week gains the reward of good health. The student who studies every day, even for a small period of time, is the one who shines through in all tests and examinations. The individual who works diligently every day earns prosperity. The employee who works one mile extra every day achieves success. An artist who practices his art for some time every day creates a masterpiece. The seeker who contemplates every day succeeds in unraveling all of life's secrets.

The basic principle of all the world's disciplines is consistency. Those who work diligently become successful. To achieve this success, you must develop the quality of consistency and create your identity as someone who is focused and persistent.

A man once embarked on a quest of a famous treasure. With only some maps and books with him, he set out and soon found himself climbing a mountain. While climbing he encountered heavy rain and lightning, due to which the climb was slippery and difficult. Facing such difficulties, he began searching for a safe place like a cave to sit and study his maps and books. He prayed for a safe and dry place, and as he climbed further he saw a huge boulder rolling down the mountain heading straight for him. Quickly he jumped aside and made it out of the way in the nick of time. The boulder rolled down and stopped just a short distance away. He was relieved and couldn't help wondering what would have happened if the rock had hit him. With all the hardships and uncertainty, he gave up his pursuit and chose to return home.

He did this because he did not know the secret that where had the boulder come from. Actually, there was a cave higher up and no one had seen it before since the mouth of the cave was covered by this boulder. When the man prayed for a place to sit and study his maps, the prayer was answered and the boulder moved. Prayers have power. Prayers can move mountains. The rock moved, rolled down the mountain, and the cave was revealed. If the man had known the importance of consistency, he would have continued and reached the cave. The rock came hurtling towards him so that his desire for a safe place to study the maps would increase. However, he gave up his quest.

We make the same mistake in our own lives. We give up when we see the boulders of problems coming at us. Problems are meant to teach us strength and to increase the desire for our goal. We grow stronger by facing adversities. If someone prays for success but loses his job, he then finds the strength to start his own business and becomes more successful than before. It is this strength that makes us self-reliant.

People make the mistake of focusing on the problem more than required. They lose themselves in negative thinking and hopelessness surrounds them. Because of hopelessness, the solution that was on the way stops in its tracks. Those who know the secret of consistency continue to persevere and make progress. In this process they learn the secret of how their prayers are fulfilled. They contemplate to understand the problem and then immediately shift their focus on solutions. This is what helps them to progress on the path of success. You must shift your focus from problems and bring it into present awareness. The solutions are in this moment.

When you persist with your efforts, a time will come when the boulders of difficulties will move from their place and charge towards you. Don't fear them, they are actually auspicious. Remember, difficulties come to give you strength.

Demosthenes, a renowned orator from ancient Greek, used to stammer and stutter while speaking. To fulfil his dream of becoming a great public speaker, he decided to do something about his problem. He started to practice speaking by placing a marble in his mouth. To make sure that his face did not distort while speaking, he would stand in front of a mirror. He would speak while running on mountains so as to increase his stamina and lung capacity. In order to speak loudly at public gatherings, he would practice speaking over the splashing sounds of the sea. Due to his relentless efforts and consistent practice, he overcame his stutter and became one of Greece's greatest orators.

This book presents to you 7 spiritual secrets and 7 steps to transform failure into a blessing. If your mind starts making excuses in applying them, remind it the mantra: *A little, but today*. Choose the right thoughts, actions, and qualities. Write them in a diary and work on them every day bit by bit, starting today. If you decide to exercise five days a week, stick to this resolution, no matter what. This is consistency. When you set your mind to work with consistency, you get thoughts of inspired action, and you achieve even bigger goals. If such thoughts do not occur, continue to develop the capability of your body, mind, and intellect. Let go of false beliefs regarding failure and success, and continue with voice of faith and forgiveness prayer, so that you become receptive to thoughts of inspired action… transformation can happen at any moment. When water is heated consistently, the temperature slowly reaches 100 degrees Celsius, and the water turns into steam. It becomes so powerful that it can run a steam engine. This is transformation. Hence work on developing your qualities with consistency and you will surely succeed.

Decoding nature's clues

Let us understand this with the help of an example.

Southern regions of America had good production of cotton. Farmers would always grow cotton but once upon a time their plants became infected with some disease and the crops were completely destroyed. Thereafter the farmers unwillingly chose to grow the crop of soya bean and peanuts. They also started to rear animals.

As a result, their profits increased manifold and they were more successful.

This means a seemingly negative event can yield positive results. It can teach us something new and redirect our course to something better. Thus, sometimes a failure or a setback may be an indication that we need to change our direction or our field. Nature gives us clues and indications; we should learn to identify and understand them, and work accordingly.

Suppose a person who has never exercised in his life, falls ill. This illness is indicating towards the action course of exercise. Sometimes we don't know which qualities we need to develop and when. Nature creates certain circumstances in which certain qualities are required to face the situation. One who identifies such indications for action and redirects his efforts and actions, is the one who reaches the pinnacle of success.

Breaking free of one's comfort zone

You can develop qualities and capability of your body, mind, and intellect to its fullest only if you break out of your comfort zone. Each of us is bound in the cocoon of a comfort zone in some aspect of our life. We cannot break free of it due to ignorance.

Comfort zone implies the limits of the mind and body beyond which you feel discomfort while working. It can be regarding people, place, work, or time. You are comfortable with only certain people, places, activities, or time periods. This zone is created by your own belief systems. If you do not try to break these false beliefs, you are unable to explore your maximum potential. All your powers remain unmanifested.

Comfort zone regarding time means owing to certain false beliefs you lose the desire to work further after a certain time period due to loss of enthusiasm or energy. Both the mind and the body resist work and do not wish to step out of the comfort zone. Due to this habit, you are unable to grow. You are unable to break the boundaries of your comfort zone, even if you wish to. For example, a student, who studies for a few hours and stops after reaching the limits of his comfort zone, is unable to discover his latent talents and skills.

Our day is over in just managing the activities related to our school, college, office, or home. Due to this, our life will continue to be the same as it has always been. If you wish to attain special success, you need to break free of your comfort zone and do something different after your routine activities, such as:

1. Even if the mind is reluctant, meet new people and discuss things with them.

2. To learn something new, invest some time, efforts, and money, even if initially your mind may not agree for such an investment.

3. After you feel tired and before you stop working, continue to work for 5-10 minutes more.

4. Write something. Stories, poems, or articles for a newspaper, magazine, or website. Write letters or emails to people of different countries. This will help you to gain worldwide information.

5. Read motivational and self-help books to build your confidence. Be a member of a library or a spiritual group.

6. Experiment with new things, like teach your neighborhood children, repair machines at home, paint, draw, sing, or organize events.

7. Accept an invitation to give a speech. Take it as a challenge if you are uncomfortable with it.

8. Spend an entire day with eyes closed. It might reveal to you things of which you were not aware of earlier.

In the beginning these activities may seem very unpleasant but it will help to rupture your comfort zone. Soon you will be amazed to discover so many qualities and powers that were lying dormant within you.

Identifying the opportunity

If you have decided to develop qualities, inculcate virtues, and upgrade skills, then every event serves as an opportunity. Thus, there are so many opportunities in life to do so. However, since we are unable to identify the opportunity, we lose out on these precious chances and instead get caught up in unhappiness and unrest. If an unpleasant event occurs, our internal harmony gets shaken. Peace gives way to blames and complaints: "Why did I fail, it's not fair, it is so humiliating..."

If we accept that however unpleasant a situation is, it can be converted into an opportunity to learn; then we will enjoy both the positive and the negative situations. We will be aware of the fact that a disagreeable situation has arisen not to give us pain but to teach us something.

You will see many such examples around you, where, an unpleasant event yielded good results. For example, someone lost a job, and started a business out of necessity. As the months passed by, he became a successful entrepreneur. He could have plunged into dejection. Thus, we should realize that more the awareness of opportunity, more will be chances of success. Examine in your life, how many such opportunities you were able to identify and how many of them went unidentified.

If someone had to suffer severe economic constraints, and if that person learns to live prudently, then he will forever get rid of financial problems. Those who have a habit of leaving tasks undone can enjoy lifelong success if they learn time management. If someone's relationships are entangled in misunderstandings, then learning human relations and good communication can help one to enjoy warm and harmonious relations throughout life.

Meditation for developing qualities

First read the entire meditation points given below and internalize it. Then practice it every day to develop qualities as soon as possible.

1. Close your eyes and focus on your heart region. Believe that you have the power to be complete and perfect.
2. Every creation of God has at least one virtue. Since a human being is God's supreme creation, each one of us is a treasure house of divine qualities. All the best qualities are innately present within us. Visualize the blooming and blossoming of all your qualities and powers.
3. Every person is the manifest form of the formless God. Hence, always identify and focus on the virtues and qualities in others.
4. As soon as you focus on others' qualities, your attention gives energy to those qualities and enhances them. Thus, observe only virtues and qualities in people, plants, animals, flowers, thorns, living, non-living, and everything in the universe.
5. Additionally, just by observation, those very qualities lying dormant within you will awaken. Hence bring each relative and friend one by one before your mind's eye. Identify their qualities and contemplate on them.
6. Develop the habit of admiring the qualities in others and say to God, "Thank You for _____" (those qualities). Gratitude

brings a feeling of completeness. This feeling of completeness acts like a magnet for those qualities.

7. Always focus on, contemplate, praise, and thank the Creator for these qualities: steadfast, obedient, pure, loving, and unwavering mind, fearlessness, capability, completing jobs successfully, feeling of abundance, acceptance, taking responsibility, ease in every activity, amiability, unbreakable faith, benevolence, firmness, foresightedness, courage, self-respect, honesty, total growth, inspiration, endless energy, *viveka*, efficiency, creativity, listening to your heart, etc.

8. Allow the fundamental attributes of love, bliss, and stillness to awaken within you.

9. Feel that with the power of love, bliss, and stillness, you are able to observe, praise, and thank the divine qualities that you observe in others.

10. See yourself developing all the positive qualities with the power of love, joy, and stillness.

11. Chant for 2-3 minutes: Love, joy, stillness… Love, joy, stillness… Love, joy, stillness…

SUMMARY:

1. Success and qualities go hand in hand. Hence, always focus on enhancing your qualities.

2. According to Law of Focus, *what you focus on, increases.* Any quality can be imbibed by focusing on it.

3. Always keep your focus on the one whom you consider your ideal. This will activate the development of all the virtues within you that your ideal has.

4. If your goal is grand, then you must be patient and persistent until you achieve it.

5. The magical power of patience can be summed up as: WATCH, WAIT with WONDER!

6. Consistency is the fundamental quality that helps you to develop other qualities or skills.

7. A seemingly negative event can yield positive results; it can teach you something new and redirect your course to something better. One who identifies such indications from nature and redirects his efforts and actions, is the one who reaches the pinnacle of success.

8. You can develop qualities and capability of your body, mind, and intellect to its fullest only if you break out of your comfort zone.

9. If you have decided to develop qualities, inculcate virtues, and upgrade skills, then every event serves as an opportunity.

10. Since a human being is God's supreme creation, all the best qualities are innately present within you. They just need to be awakened through the power of observation, focus, contemplation, and gratitude.

* * *

An important key to success is self-confidence.
An important key to self-confidence is preparation.
— Arthur Ashe

VOICE OF FAITH
FOR FINAL SUCCESS

Miracles are occurring every day in this world.
I am ready for my divine plan.
I am eliminating all negative thoughts.
I am letting the divine power that controls
the sun, moon, and planets to work through me.
Life is for me.
I march ahead with love, joy and faith
because I know that success and abundance
are flowing towards everyone.

Step 6

UNDERSTANDING

Understanding is the torch on the path of supreme success.

To attain success that lies beyond the duality of failure and success, what one needs is 'understanding'. Use the weapon of understanding to slay the demon of ignorance. This means you need to shed your tendencies, bad habits, and old thinking patterns in order to think what no can think, to see what no one can see, and to create what people need but aren't yet aware of.

The biggest obstacle in 'understanding' is ignorance and unconsciousness. Due to these two factors, we are not able to understand what and how we should seek. Sometimes, owing to ignorance, we tend to ask for that which proves to be harmful. Let us understand this with a story.

A bird was flying from one country to another during its migration period. It was icy cold due to which the bird froze and fell to the ground. A cow was passing by and left a big heap of dung over the bird's little body. The bird was furious with the cow and starting cursing it. However, the warmth of the cow dung raised its body temperature and its shivering reduced. The bird was able to move a bit. Just then a cat happened to pass by. Seeing the movement, the cat tried to investigate the matter. But due to the big heap of dung, it could not find anything and started walking away. The bird thought, "Someone had come to help, but was unable to see me." It started lamenting aloud, "O God, this is not fair! First you froze me and then smacked me with cow dung. How can you do this?!" As soon as the cat heard the bird's voice, it returned and ate up the bird.

Sometimes events in life are paradoxical. The bird thought that being heaped with cow dung is bad, yet it's the dung that saved its life but the bird could not understand this. And then it felt that the cat was going to help, but instead the cat killed it.

Thus, what needs to be understood is that failures in life may not be failures at all, they could be a blessing in disguise.

This story shows how to look at events occurring throughout the world from the highest perspective. Do not immediately apply labels such as 'this is good' and 'that is bad'. Stop for a while and contemplate, otherwise you may not be able to ask for the right things, and instead end up harming yourself.

Kindle the torch of understanding right now and pledge to break all your patterns and tendencies. Else, even after attaining the highest, you may get stuck in the desire for inferior things only because of a tendency. Let's understand this with the example of a security guard.

Once a genie appeared before a security guard and was ready to fulfil any of his three wishes. According to his first wish, the genie transported him to a big city. Then he wished for the world's biggest and the most beautiful bungalow. The genie fulfilled that too. Then the genie asked about his third wish. The guard said, "Now make me the security guard of this bungalow."

After the fulfillment of his first two big wishes, what did the guard ask for? To become a guard again! This was his tendency. We should not make the same mistake and hence we need to eradicate each one of our tendencies. Otherwise, even after understanding 'Failure is the stepping stone to success,' we will go back to square one due to our old tendency and start cursing failure. This is the biggest obstacle in attaining success.

If you are about to begin a project, then as per the principle of understanding, you need to think over it, plan it, and execute it using the 5 maxims given below. These maxims will prevent failure, and if you are facing failure, then they will help you in overcoming it and achieving success.

Maxim 1: Foresightedness

To develop complete understanding, foresightedness is vital. This quality helps you to see in the present all the possibilities that can occur in the future.

For example, if there are aches or fatigue in your body, then due to foresightedness, you would recognize it to be a harbinger of some illness and hence begin to take measures to improve your health even before the illness begins. You would probably start exercising and make changes in your diet and lifestyle. If your mind is filled with stress, then to prevent falling sick, you will carry out self-analysis and practice meditation. As a result, your mind will become calm and steady and you will feel emotionally healthier.

In earthquake zones, engineers build buildings that can withstand earthquakes. This is foresight. To create a happy, self-reliant, and highly developed society, preplanning is important. If the population is multiplying at a rapid rate, then it wouldn't be very helpful to think about water and housing issues after 5 years when the population has already exploded. It is important to make a plan and start taking practical steps in the present.

All the above examples may seem like common sense today, but they began with foresight. This is just like computers which just three decades ago were a rarity and not considered useful for the common man. Only a few people had the foresight to see that computers will become a household tool. Foresightedness is indeed a rare quality and very few people have it. Those few who have it are able to perceive possibilities of the future with contemplation. They can see the scenario some years forward, based on the present situation. For instance, if the society is moving in a particular direction, what would be the scenario after 10 years and what needs to be done in the present, to prepare for those possibilities? Consequently, even if unwanted situations appear, these foresighted people are not disturbed, since they have the solutions ready with them. They live successfully even through difficult times.

Foresightedness means to work on present indications to prepare for the future. It does not mean you have to keep thinking about the future pointlessly, which creates stress. But if you think with foresight, there will be no room for stress or worry. Foresightedness should help to improve the present, and if the present is good, then the future will certainly shape up beautifully.

Maxim 2: Investing for the future

Investment for the future goes hand in hand with foresightedness. We should ask ourself, "What changes can I bring in my life today that will be beneficial for my future? What investments can I make today?" By combining foresightedness with investment for the future, you will flourish over time and make great progress. Here we are not speaking about money alone.

Let's assume a person exercises for 10 minutes at present. He can decide to add 2 more minutes per month in this daily exercise routine. Similarly, if one is investing 10 minutes in meditation every day, then as investment for the future he can add 1 more minute per week. These extra investments may seem negligible today, but consistent additions result in tremendous benefits over time.

After six months, this person would be exercising 20 minutes and meditating for more than half an hour.

Let's drive home this point with the help of a little story.

There was a young boy who used to take care of his cattle. Among his cattle was an adorable little calf. The boy was very fond of this calf and would carry it on his shoulders while performing his routine activities. Gradually this developed into a habit. As the calf grew, the physical strength of the boy also increased in accordance to the calf's weight. Within a few years, the calf had grown into a full-size bull and still the boy could easily carry it on his shoulders! Thus, his seed of strength slowly grew into an astonishing feat, without paying much attention to it and without putting in any extra effort.

We too should think over what small actions (tantamount to sowing seeds) can be introduced in our present that can yield maximum fruit in our future without much attention. This habit is synonymous to our childhood piggybanks. You are encouraged to save coins in the piggybank whenever possible, and after some period when you break it open, you are astonished to find so many coins. In the same way, regular investment of small actions today can lead to mammoth results in the future.

Maxim 3: Think It Through

When you have undertaken a big project, the third aspect to unravel the principle of understanding is to contemplate the project from all possible angles and perspectives so as to comprehend its full depth. In order to do so, it is very helpful to consider other stakeholders' viewpoints too. Brainstorming sessions should be conducted; and sometimes it is amazing to witness each member coming up with an angle which the others have not even thought of. Such sessions bring to light all the factors related to the event or project.

This is crucial because when you are planning for a big event or a long term project, it is highly effective to have a check-list of its every aspect. To prepare a check-list, first divide the project or event into smaller tasks. Arrange these tasks in various categories so that it is easier to contemplate over them. Then bring together all the categories to form the master plan. Lastly, arrange all the tasks in chronological order so that it is clear which task is to be done when. This process is called 'Think it through', which means visualizing each step of the project from beginning to end. This will help in completing the project smoothly and successfully.

Maxim 4: Awareness of long term goal

When we divide a project into smaller parts, then during their analysis and execution, our focus should be on what qualities we can develop in the long term during the process. Thus, we would not be limited to short term goals of the project but also focus on the overall picture. This long term goal, in fact, should be imprinted in the minds of every member involved in the project.

Ask this very important question truthfully to yourself: "Why am I involved in this project?" Determine the purpose of every action that you do. Else, at the end of the work, you may be overcome with doubt whether you did the right thing or not.

While executing a project, keeping the goal in mind helps you to remember the long term benefits. This helps you to focus not only on completing the project but also to use it as an opportunity for learning. It will help you to build those abilities which will later help you to grow spiritually as well. Your perspective regarding your work will widen and deepen.

Maxim 5: Trustworthiness

While working on a project, event, job, or even while running your own business, it is important to understand the value of trustworthiness in order to attain success as well as to maintain success.

While chatting with his assistant, a manager wondered, "Do you think this project would be completed on time?" His assistant said, "First tell me, to whom are you going to assign this project?" The manager informed, "I'm thinking of either Atul or Mohit for this project." The assistant replied confidently, "If you give it to Atul, he will definitely complete it on time and in the best possible manner. But if you give it to Mohit, I doubt he'll be able to complete it on schedule because even the smallest impediment will be enough to throw him off the track."

It is clear from this conversation that Atul was considered dependable in that company, while Mohit was not. The name Atul was enough to instill confidence in the manager about the job at hand. Like Atul, you need to build your trustworthiness and credibility to such an extent that as soon as people hear your name, they are 100% sure that the job will be done. Trustworthiness is a quality that helps you gain the confidence of people. This confidence itself plays a major role in your success. And success builds up even more confidence.

To find out your reliability quotient, close your eyes for a minute and reflect upon the following: "Do people trust me and have confidence in me? To what extent? Do I fulfill my commitments? Or do I forget to honor my commitments? When my name comes up for a job, what does it evoke in people's minds—confidence or doubt? Can people trust me with any responsibility?"

People's faith in you makes you indebted to them. When you break someone's trust, your interest mounts, but when you fulfill the responsibility, you are paying back the premium. It does not matter how big or small a task is. These accounts are being calculated in the invisible realm. Since people are unable to see such calculations, they fall short of people's faith in them.

People who honor their commitments and live up to expectations are able to go about their jobs easily and accomplish their goals smoothly. Everyone likes such people, due to which they are always in demand and there is no shortage of work for them.

A thief was once asked, "You have been stealing for so many years. Why haven't you picked up an accomplice to help you increase your business?" The thief's solemn reply was: "I want to, but where would I find someone totally trustworthy?"

Thus, even thieves wish for trustworthy people as accomplices. Everyone needs reliable people.

To evaluate your own reliability, ask yourself, "If I were the owner of a company, would I hire people like me?" Since you know your own nature and tendencies very well, you will also know the answer. By asking yourself such questions, you can instantly find out your own shortcomings, weaknesses, and in what ways you are not dependable.

Given below are the steps you can take to become totally trustworthy:

- First of all, start trusting yourself and live up to that trust. This means, make certain commitments to yourself and fulfill those commitments. See yourself as a trustworthy person through the eyes of your mind. Then with full faith, start taking steps towards this goal.

- Learn to trust others. Start appreciating the reliability that you see in others. The Law of Focus will then start working. By focusing on reliability, you will start imbibing it.

- It is important to develop self-discipline in order to become trustworthy. One who has a strong body and balanced mind finds it easy to surpass any benchmark of trustworthiness. Hence develop self-discipline with balanced food intake, good control over your senses, exercising your body and mind, and giving the right direction to your thoughts. If one cannot take care of one's body and mind and falls prey to illnesses and excuses, then it is difficult to become reliable for any project. Laziness makes you procrastinate today's task to tomorrow. When the deadline is missed, you not only have to apologize but also your reliability goes down.

- Make a list of 'things to do' and try to complete it on schedule. All your wrong habits like laziness, procrastination, carelessness, fear, etc. will come to the fore in this process. Despite these obstacles, put in all your efforts to complete everything in the list on time. This will raise your dependability in your own eyes. You will become more confident. Don't forget to pat your back after ticking off each item in the list.

- Repeat to yourself the intention: "I am complete. Everything gets completed by me on time." With this mantra, take the intention of completing every task that you undertake. The feeling of completeness and fulfillment boosts self-discipline and willpower.

- Speak clearly, honestly, and politely with people. The ability to do so plays a major role in gaining their trust. Resolve never to play down or exaggerate things, twist or hide facts, or beat around the bush while speaking to people. Never make false promises. If you don't fulfil your promises, you lose your trustworthiness and cause harm to yourself.

- If it is not possible for you to do something, politely say so in clear words. For example, you may say, "I would have loved to do it, but due to prior commitments I am unable to take this responsibility. My sincere apologies!" People won't be offended. In fact, they will respect you for being frank and honest.

- Abstain from gossiping and talking behind someone's back. Sooner or later, people come to know what you had been talking about them. It immediately diminishes their trust upon you. Thus, these habits are harmful for you as well as others.

- Keep confidential matters confidential. You definitely need to develop this quality to become trustworthy. Many a time it is important to keep some matters confidential, especially in an office setting. If you are able to do it, you gain the trust of your seniors. Even in relations, people sometimes pour their hearts out and confide in you. You need to keep such matters to yourself, else you will completely lose their trust.

A little girl and her father were walking across a shaky bridge. The father said, "Child, hold my hand or else you might fall." The girl thought for a moment and said, "No, Dad! You hold my hand because I may lose my grip. But I know that no matter what happens you will never let go of me."

Such trustworthiness is what you should aim for. Become trustworthy not just for one person but for the whole world. If you take the steps given above, your feelings, thoughts, words, and actions will harmonize to collectively make you trustworthy. Remember that you will be given higher responsibilities only if you are reliable. And with higher responsibilities, you will be able to explore and achieve your highest potential. Every day, life is providing you opportunities to become trustworthy. Grab these opportunities because reliability opens the doors to supreme success.

SUMMARY:

1. To gain success that lies beyond the duality of failure and success, what's required is 'understanding'.
2. Shed your tendencies, bad habits, and old thinking patterns in order to think what no can think, to see what no one can see, and to create what people need but aren't yet aware of.

3. Do not immediately apply labels to events as good or bad. Stop for a while and contemplate, otherwise you may not be able to ask for the right things, and instead end up harming yourself.

4. Kindle the torch of understanding right now and pledge to break all your patterns and tendencies. Else, even after attaining the highest, you may get stuck in the desire for inferior things only because of a tendency.

5. Foresightedness means to work on present indications to prepare for the future. This will help you to live successfully even through difficult times.

6. Regular investment of small actions today can lead to mammoth results in the future, even without much effort or attention.

7. 'Think it through' means visualizing each step of the project from beginning to end.

8. During the analysis and execution of a project, our focus should be on what qualities we can develop in the long term during the process. Thus, we would not be limited to short term goals of the project but also focus on the overall picture.

9. Everyone likes dependable people, due to which they are always in demand.

10. Trustworthiness is a quality that helps you gain the confidence of people. You will be given higher responsibilities only if you are reliable. Higher responsibilities open the doors for exploring and achieving your highest potential.

* * *

Luminous Lives

SWAMI VIVEKANANDA

"You are lions, you are souls—pure, infinite, and perfect. The might of the universe is within you."
— Swami Vivekananda

Swami Vivekananda is considered one of the chief saints of India and a great religious leader. The prime disciple of 19th century Indian mystic Ramakrishna Paramhansa, he reintroduced the Indian philosophies of Vedanta and Yoga to the Western world. His work helped in raising interfaith awareness and bringing Hinduism to the status of a major world religion during the late 19th century. He was a major force in bringing about unity among Indians and contributed to the concept of freedom and independence in colonial India.

Early Years

Vivekananda was born as Narendranath Dutta (Naren) in an affluent family of Calcutta on January 12, 1863. His father was an attorney and his mother a devout housewife. Naren's upbringing was influenced by his father's liberal thinking and his mother's spiritual and devotional temperament.

A precocious boy, Narendra excelled in music, gymnastics, and studies. He had an astonishing memory and tremendous intellectual capacity. By the time he graduated from Calcutta University, he had acquired a vast knowledge of different subjects, especially Western philosophy and history. He also had profound interest in Puranas, Vedas, and Upanishads. Born with a yogic temperament, he used to practice meditation even from his boyhood, and was associated with the Brahmo Movement for some time. At the threshold of youth, Narendra was assailed by doubts about the existence of God. That is when he first met his master Sri Ramakrishna Paramhansa. With the master's help, he grew spiritually and experienced God or Self (Self Realization). He also learnt that all living beings are an embodiment of the divine self; therefore, service to God could be rendered by service to mankind.

Difficult Situations

Narendra's father suddenly passed away in 1884. This left the family penniless and Narendra became responsible for supporting his mother and siblings. Creditors began demanding the repayment of loans and relatives threatened to evict the family from their ancestral home. Naren and his family would often go hungry. Many a day he fasted so that his family might have something to eat. This is the phase during which he understood poverty and developed true compassion for the poor.

He unsuccessfully tried to find work day after day, but refused to earn money by questionable means. One day, on Ramakrishna's suggestion, Naren went to the temple thrice and tried to pray to Goddess Kali for his family's financial welfare. However, he failed to pray for any kind of worldly necessities and ultimately prayed for divine knowledge and devotion. Ramakrishna was pleased and bestowed him with a blessing that his family would henceforth never face lack of essentials like food and clothes. Naren soon found the job of a school teacher.

Sri Ramakrishna was diagnosed with cancer of the throat. His young disciples, with Narendra as their group leader, nursed him with devoted care. With instructions from the master, a new monastic order was formed. Shortly thereafter the master passed away and Narendra founded the Ramakrishna Math. On taking formal monastic vows, Narendra became Swami Vivekananda. He felt an inner calling to spread the teachings of his master. He toured the Indian subcontinent extensively and came face-to-face with the shocking conditions prevailing in British India. Living primarily on *bhiksha* (alms), Narendra travelled sometimes by train (with tickets bought by admirers) but often on foot. In his *Completed Works*, he writes of his experience:

"Many times I have been in the jaws of death, starving, footsore, and weary. For days and days, I had no food, and often could walk no further; I would sink down under a tree, and life would seem to be ebbing away. I could not speak, I could scarcely think, but at last the mind reverted to the idea: *I have no fear nor death; never was I born, never did I die; I never hunger or thirst. I am It! I am It!"*

He found extensive suffering and poverty throughout India and resolved to uplift the nation.

Journey to the Western world

In 1893, he decided to speak at the World Parliament of Religions in Chicago to present the great teachings of Vedanta to the world as well as to seek financial help for upliftment of the masses. In America he faced a lot of ridicule and abuse from people due to his skin color and "strange" clothes. He had no money to stay or eat. In spite of severe impediments, he faced everything calmly, surrendering himself into God's hands. Some people helped him as they felt inspired by his divine words and personality. With their help, he finally reached the conference. Despite everything he had faced, he began his address with, "Sisters and brothers of America..." These words touched the heart of every member of the audience and they burst into a thunderous applause that continued for a very long time. He quoted, "As the different streams having their sources in different places all mingle their water in the sea, so, O Lord, the different paths which men take, all lead to Thee!"

Thereafter Vivekananda was loved and honored by all the delegates, the press, and everywhere he went. He was highly sought after and spent nearly two years lecturing across U.S. and also founded the Vedanta Centers for study and practice of Vedanta. He adapted traditional Hindu ideas and religiosity to suit the needs and understandings of his western audiences. In 1896 his book *Raja Yoga* was published, which became an instant success and was highly influential in the western understanding of Yoga. Vivekananda attracted many followers and admirers in the U.S. and Europe, including philosophers, psychologists, doctors, scientists, lawyers, politicians, authors, artists, etc., some of whom also contributed to his cause. Earlier, while sailing to America, Vivekananda had also inspired Jamshedji Tata to set up a research and educational institution in India.

Return to India

Vivekananda was received warmly on his return to India. He started delivering lectures in various cities, which created a great stir all over the country. He repeatedly addressed social issues: uplifting the people, eliminating the caste system, promoting science and industrialization, addressing widespread poverty, and ending colonial rule. In 1897, in Calcutta, Vivekananda founded the *Ramakrishna Mission* for social service. His nationalistic ideas influenced many Indian thinkers and leaders such as Gandhi, Tilak, Subhas Chandra Bose, and many more. His teachings gave real strength and purpose to India's nationalist movement. He played a major role in awakening the people of India and mobilizing the youth. All the rigorous activity took a toll on his health. Yet he continued to work with undying zeal in the social and spiritual spheres till the very last day of his life—a short but luminous life of just 39 years. His birthday is celebrated as the National Youth Day in

India, and the day he delivered his masterful speech at the Parliament of Religions, 11 September 1893 is celebrated as the World Brotherhood Day. Even today his teachings inspire people all over the world.

Impact on India and the World

Vivekananda opened the minds of Indians to their duty to the downtrodden masses. He elevated social service to the status of divine service. He strengthened the sense of unity among Indians and gave a proper understanding of India's great spiritual heritage and thus gave all the Indians pride in their past and inspiration to build a bright future. He brought about an overall unification of the various sects of Hinduism. He created respect for India and Hinduism in the Western world by expounding its great spiritual principles and their relevance in the modern world.

One of his most significant contributions to the modern world is his interpretation of religion as a universal experience of transcendent Reality, common to all humanity. He showed that religion and science are not contradictory to each other but are in fact complementary. This universal conception frees religion from the hold of superstitions, dogmatism, priest craft, and intolerance, and makes spirituality the highest and noblest pursuit—the pursuit of supreme freedom, supreme knowledge, and supreme happiness.

Some of his highly inspirational teachings

- You are lions, you are souls, pure, infinite, and perfect. The might of the universe is within you. "Why weepest thou, my friend?"
- It is faith that makes a lion of a man.
- All the power is within you. You can do anything and everything; believe in that. Don't believe that you are weak; stand up and express the divinity within you.

- Fill the brain with high thoughts, highest ideals, place them day and night before you, and out of that will come great work.
- Religion is the manifestation of the Divinity already in man.
- This is the gist of all worship: to be pure and to do good to others.
- Purity, patience, and perseverance are the three essentials to success, and above all, love.
- Teach yourselves, teach everyone his real nature, call upon the sleeping soul and see how it awakes. Power will come, glory will come, goodness will come, purity will come, and everything that is excellent will come when this sleeping soul is roused to Self conscious activity.

• • •

STEP 7

FINAL SUCCESS

*Realizing your divine self
and helping others to realize it too is Final Success.*

Growth and maturity in every major aspect of our life is vital, but spiritual maturity is the most important and the most essential. If you have it, then you can grow and progress in any other aspect. However, people who are living a mechanical life and always running in the rat race think that spirituality and worldly affairs lie on diagonally opposite ends. They believe that one cannot become spiritual while living a normal life fulfilling one's responsibilities and chasing material goals. This means one has to give up their present life, their desires, and dreams, if one wishes to tread the spiritual path.

Such notions about spirituality are totally wrong. The reality is that when you have grown and matured spiritually, then,

- You are able to progress and succeed in every aspect of life, and the most important thing is you are able to enjoy life at the same time.
- You do not let success go to your head.
- Failures and problems do not make you miserable, dejected, or worried.

- You are not afraid of taking decisions or calculated risks. And even if you feel afraid, you do not fear this fear; you take it in your stride as part of the process and move ahead.
- You are always ready to learn something new.
- You can adapt and move with the times.
- Your mind is focused and your intellect is capable of deep as well as subtle thinking.
- You do not get entangled in false beliefs and thoughts, and that's why you are able to fully open and blossom and lead a blissful life.
- You can easily achieve all your various goals.
- You know who you actually are, why you have come to Earth, what is the purpose of your life, what is the role of people and relations in your life, and what is the ultimate aim beyond all your aims.
- After knowing the truth, you become capable of giving your 100% to every situation without getting stuck in any event.
- You become flexible and live life beyond the duality of failure and success.
- No ill-will or envy remains in your mind. You emanate positive energy and vibes.
- You are flexible in your relationships rather than headstrong, and thereby there is harmony and warmth in all your familial, social, and professional relations.

In a nutshell, if you grow spiritually, you become capable of achieving your highest potential in every aspect of life. Spiritual maturity can be developed by listening to the truth, reading and contemplating the truth, and by being in the company of people who are treading the path of truth.

Thus, you can cruise to success by making yourself physically, mentally, intellectually, and spiritually capable, and facing the unsuccessful areas of your life head on. Seven secrets and seven steps have been presented to you in this book that will help in enhancing your capability. These will prove to be the milestones in your journey that will take you beyond the duality of failure and success, and establish you in the realm of Final Success.

Final Success

After being born on Earth, becoming human is the first success and becoming divine is final success. Realizing our formless divine nature and getting established in it is final success. The bridge between the first and the final success is 'capability'. The secrets and steps presented in all the previous chapters will increase your capability. As your capability rises, you will move towards the peak of success.

In general, success makes us happy and failure plunges us into misery. Appreciation tickles us, while criticism makes us cringe. Comfort and convenience pleases us, while inconvenience causes distress. This is the web of nature, the *maya*, the illusory world of duality. We can attain final success only after liberation from this duality.

All living beings, including plants, animals, as well as human beings are stuck in the cycle of nature. Only humans have the possibility to work their way out of this cycle. Animals give birth to their younger ones during the breeding period, feed them, and after sometime leave them to live independently. These younger ones after growing up follow the same cycle. Each living being is bound by this cycle and cannot escape it.

Only human beings have two options. They can either spend their life unhappily following nature's cycle, or lead a truly successful life by stepping out of this cycle. This is what makes human beings supreme among all living beings. It is stated in mythologies that even gods wish to take birth as human beings. They too want to come to Earth and practice combating failures. In order to raise their level of consciousness, they wish to take some challenges, which is possible only through the human body.

Eating, drinking, entertaining, enjoying comforts and luxuries can be done within the purview of nature's cycle. But this is not the only purpose of human birth. Upon overcoming these desires, it is possible to realize our true self, get established in it, and express our divine qualities through this very body. This is why the human body is considered extremely precious. It is through this body that one can break out of nature's cycle and express one's true nature.

When a rocket is released from Earth, it requires extra power or boosters to break out of the gravitational field of Earth. Once it is out of this field, boosters are not required and its journey becomes easier as the attraction towards its destination overtakes it. Similarly, in the beginning you need extra strength to escape nature's cycle. This strength will help you to make decisions and take actions that are against your innate tendencies. This strength, this capability is the secret to success.

Animals do not have this possibility and are bound to lead a defined and limited life in accordance with nature's cycle. Those people who have the desire to attain real success rise above animal existence. Otherwise, man is simply an animal with a human body. Those individuals who develop some awareness are able to observe that they are behaving in a particular manner because they are stuck in the cycle of duality and in nature's cycle, and this means they belong to the category of animals. Those who come out of these cycles become human beings in the true sense. The first condition to overcome failure is to become human.

It is not enough to have a human form. In the coming years, the rapid development of science will make it possible to give human form to animals and make one animal look like another. But we know that even if a goat looks like a lion, it doesn't mean that it becomes a lion, because from inside it is scared just like a goat. However, this scenario does not belong only to the future. This has been going on since ages. People look like humans but are actually not; they haven't risen above the level of beasts. Hence we need to honestly ask ourselves: "What is my level? What am I living as? How much have I raised my level?"

The basis of your success or failure is your decisions. That is why you need to take every decision with awareness. Ask yourself, "What do I consider myself while taking a decision? Do I consider myself as merely a body or as my true divine self?" Attachment to the body should be only to the extent that is essential to keep it functional. The body is merely the medium for experiencing and expressing your true self; which is the main purpose of your life.

One might say, "I have grown to be such a successful person. I own a company and have been on foreign tours several times. I take BIG decisions and they turn out to be accurate most of the times." An individual can prove a lot about what he or she is by displaying their material success. But when they examine within, they will realize that the basis of all their decisions was either greed or fear, which belong to the realm of illusion. All decisions were taken with the belief that they are the body and for providing comforts and luxuries for this body. However, the reality is that the body is simply a mirror to experience our formless self. We should be attached to the body only to the extent that it will help us to witness our true self. The mirror should simply work as a mirror. Do not let your decisions be based upon decorating the mirror.

If you believe that you are the body, then all your decisions will be taken based on this belief, such as how to make your body beautiful, how to make your body live longer, how to make your body immortal, and so on. Various medicines and herbs are sought to add more years to one's life. Trying to discover medicines and herbs for good health is fine, but so much emphasis is being given to living a very long life, to become immortal. But has anybody thought what will they do by living for say 200 or 300 years? What decisions will the leaders take after staying alive for 300 years and what will be its consequences upon the world?! The fact is that even if a few thoughtful people take the right decisions, there is a possibility of heralding a beautiful transformation of this planet.

The body's health should be maintained, it should be taken care of, but only as a medium. If you eat more than what is required to satisfy hunger or indulge excessively in sensual pleasures, it means that the claws of illusion have sunk in deep and you are severely stuck in nature's cycle.

Your decisions are your mirror. If decisions are taken due to ambition, vices, ego, or desires, it indicates that nature's cycle or the web of illusion has a firm hold upon you. You will focus merely on breeding and keeping your family tree and your species alive. Your role ends there. You won't be able to do anything more. A Hindu will give birth to more Hindus and a Muslim will give birth to more Muslims. But will he become a human? He can, if he attains wisdom and applies it. Are you going to fail in fulfilling your purpose of coming to Earth? Are you going to fail in attaining final success? Don't let that happen because you have the possibility of attaining your ultimate purpose, you can awaken and get established in your divine nature.

Now take the decision: of exploring your highest possibility… of augmenting your capability and evolving from a human being to a divine being… of moving from first success to final success.

Unlimited and Unbroken Bliss

Throughout the book, we have seen how to change your perspective towards failure and take steps to progress on the path of success. But what does success mean to you?

1. Is it achieving what you want? For example, you wanted to become an artist and you became one.
2. Is it achieving what people think as success? A high-flying job, a plush office, a big house, and rich friends, without which life is deemed a failure.
3. Is it developing all your inner powers and skills, due to which no success is unattainable for you?

There are people who have attained either or all of the above-mentioned successes. Yet they feel incomplete within. They don't feel true joy and bliss. So, what is missing? What's missing is realizing your true limitless self and your true potential. That is Final Success. You are filled with unbroken bliss and joy on attaining Final Success.

Thus, when you attain material success, develop your inner skills and powers, and also realize your true divine self, it is complete success. This is what every human being actually wants.

So, is this the final frontier? Is this the maximum extent of the happiness that you can experience? Is there no more success that can be attained beyond complete success? If you are interested, let's ask this question to Success itself. We all want success, but we never think about what Success wants. So, what does Success want—that will push your bliss and success level to the maximum?

Success wants you to express the qualities of your divine self in order to share your bliss with others and inspire them to achieve final success too. This is the second aspect of Final Success; the first being realizing your divine self and getting established in it.

Thus, help others in any way you can, without taking credit. Help people to achieve complete success. Enlighten them about their innate divinity and remind them of the immense powers hidden inside them. This is what will make your heart revel in the feeling of completeness and total fulfilment. This is what will push your happiness meter to 100%. Any other accomplishment simply cannot take you to the peak of happiness. But shifting from a personal life to an impersonal life will. You will be overflowing with love and joy.

Now, you decide what kind of success you want. Then go ahead and apply all the secrets, steps, and laws presented in this book to attain it. And don't aim small. Aim BIG. Because whatever you decide—small or big—YOU WILL ACHIEVE IT.

SUMMARY:

1. With spiritual maturity, you learn who you actually are, why you have come to Earth, what is the purpose of your life, what is the role of people and relations in your life, and what is the ultimate aim beyond all your aims.

2. By growing spiritually, you become capable of achieving your highest potential in every aspect of life. And you are able to enjoy life at the same time.

3. Spiritual maturity can be developed by listening to the truth, reading and contemplating the truth, and by being in the company of people who are treading the path of truth.

4. After being born on Earth, becoming human is the first success and realizing our divine nature and getting established in it is Final Success.

5. The bridge between the first and the final Success is 'capability'. As your capability rises, you will move towards the peak of success.

6. Only human beings have two options. They can either spend their life unhappily following nature's cycle, or lead a truly successful life by stepping out of this cycle.

7. Ask yourself, "What do I consider myself while taking a decision? Do I consider myself as merely a body or as my true divine self?"

8. When you attain material success, develop your inner skills and powers, and also realize your true self, it is complete success.

9. Success wants you to express the qualities of your divine self in order to share your bliss with others and inspire them to achieve complete success too.

10. Help others in any way you can. Enlighten people about their divine nature and the immense powers hidden inside them. This is what will make your heart revel in the feeling of completeness and total fulfilment.

* * *

You can send your opinion or feedback on this book to :

Tejgyan Foundation, Pimpri Colony, P. O. Box 25, Pimpri, Pune – 411017 (Maharashtra), INDIA
email : mail@tejgyan.com

Write for Us

We welcome writers, translators and editors to join our team. If you would like to volunteer, please email us at: englishbooks@tejgyan.org or call : +91 90110 10963 or +91 90110 13207

APPENDIX

About Sirshree

Sirshree's spiritual quest which began during his childhood, led him on a journey through various schools of thought and meditation practices. His overpowering desire to attain the truth made him relinquish his teaching job. After a long period of contemplation, his spiritual quest culminated in the attainment of the ultimate truth. Sirshree says, **"All paths that lead to the truth begin differently, but end in the same way—with understanding. Understanding is the whole thing. Listening to this understanding is enough to attain the truth."**

Sirshree is the author of several spiritual books. His books have been translated in more than 10 languages and published by leading publishers such as Penguin and Hay House.

He is the founder of Tej Gyan Foundation, a not-for-profit organization committed to raising mass consciousness by spreading "Happy Thoughts" with branches in the United States, India, Europe and Asia-Pacific. Sirshree's retreats have transformed the lives of thousands and his teachings have inspired various social initiatives for raising global consciousness.

His works include more than 100 books and 3000 discourses. Various luminaries such as His Holiness the Dalai Lama, publishers Reid Tracy and Tami Simon and yoga master Dr. B. K. S Iyengar have released Sirshree's books and lauded his work. His book *The Warrior's Mirror*, published by Penguin, was featured in the Limca Book of Records for being released on the same day in 10 languages.

Tejgyan... The Road Ahead

What is Tejgyan?

Tejgyan is the existential wisdom of the ultimate truth, which is beyond duality. In today's world, there are people who feel disharmony and are desperately trying to achieve balance in an unpredictable life. Tejgyan helps them in harmonizing with their true nature, the Self, thereby restoring balance in all aspects of their life.

And then there are those who are successful but feel a sense of emptiness or void within. Tejgyan provides them fulfillment and helps them to embark on a journey towards self-realization. There are others who feel lost and are seeking the meaning of life. Tejgyan helps them to realize the true purpose of human life.

All this is possible with Tejgyan due to a very simple reason. The experience of the ultimate truth is always available. The direct experience of this truth is possible provided the right method is known. Tejgyan is that method, that understanding. At Tej Gyan Foundation, Sirshree imparts this understanding through a System for Wisdom – a series of retreats that guides participants step by step

Magic of Awakening Retreat

Magic of Awakening is the flagship self-realization retreat offered by Tej Gyan Foundation The retreat is conducted in two languages – Hindi and English. The teachings of the retreat are non-denominational (secular).

This residential retreat is held for 3-5 days at the foundation's MaNaN Ashram amidst the glory of mountains and the pristine beauty of nature. This ashram is located at the outskirts of the city of Pune in India, and is well connected by air, road and rail. The retreat is also held at other centres of Tej Gyan Foundation across the world.

Participate in the *Magic of Awakening* retreat to attain ageless wisdom through a unique simple 'System for Wisdom' so that you can:

1. Live from pure and still presence allowing the natural qualities of consciousness, viz. peace, love, joy, compassion, abundance and creativity to manifest.

2. Acquire simple tools to use in everyday life which help quieten the chattering mind, revealing your true nature.

3. Get practical techniques to access pure presence at will and connect to the source of all answers (the inner guru).

4. Discover missing links in practices of meditation *(dhyana)*, action *(karma)*, wisdom *(gyana)* and devotion *(bhakti)*.

5. Understand the nature of your body-mind mechanism to attain freedom from tendencies and patterns.

6. Learn practical methods to shift from mind-centred living to consciousness-centred living.

For retreats contact +919921008060 or email: mail@tejgyan.com

A Mini retreat is also conducted, especially for teens (14-17 years) during summer and winter vacations

MaNaN Ashram

Survey No. 43, Sanas Nagar, Nandoshi gaon, Kirkatwadi Phata, Sinhagad Road, Dist. Pune 411024, Maharashtra, India.

About Tej Gyan Foundation

Tej Gyan Foundation (TGF) was established with the mission of creating a highly evolved society through all-round self development of every individual that transforms all the facets of his/her life. It is a non-profit organization founded on the teachings of Sirshree. The foundation has received the ISO certification (ISO 9001:2015) for its system of imparting wisdom. It has centres all across India as well as in other countries. The motto of Tej Gyan Foundation is 'Happy Thoughts'.

TGF is creating a highly evolved society through:

- Tejgyan Programs (Retreats, Courses, Television and Radio Programs, Podcasts)

- Tejgyan Products (Books, Tapes, Audio/Video CDs)

- Tejgyan Projects (Value Education, Women Empowerment, Peace Initiatives)

TGF undertakes projects to elevate the level of consciousness among students, youth, women, senior citizens, teachers, doctors, leaders, organizations, police force, prisoners, etc.

Now you can register **online** for the following retreats

Maha Aasmani Niwasi Shivir
(5 Days Residential Retreat in Hindi)

Magic of Awakening Retreat
(3 Days Residential Retreat In English)

Mini Maha Aasmani Shivir
3 Days (Residential) Retreat for Teens

🔍 www.tejgyan.org

Books can be delivered at your doorstep by registered post or courier. You can request for the same through postal money order or pay by VPP. Please send the money order to either of the following two addresses:

WOW Publishings Pvt. Ltd.

1. Registered Office: E-4, Vaibhav Nagar, Near Tapovan Mandir, Pimpri, Pune 411017.

2. Post Box No. 36, Pimpri Colony Post Office, Pimpri, , Pune 411017

Phone No. : 9011013210 / 9623457873

You can also order your copy at the online store:

www.gethappythoughts.org

*Free Shipping plus 10% Discount on purchases above Rs. 300/-.

For further details contact:

Tejgyan Global Foundation

Registered Office:
Happy Thoughts Building, Vikrant Complex, Near Tapovan Mandir, Pimpri, Pune 411017, Maharashtra, India.
Contact No: 020-27411240, 27412576
Email: mail@tejgyan.com

MaNaN Ashram:
Survey No. 43, Sanas Nagar, Nandoshi gaon, Kirkatwadi Phata, Sinhagad Road, Tal. Haveli, Dist. Pune 411024, Maharashtra, India.
Contact No: 992100 8060.

Hyderabad: 9885558100, **Bangalore:** 9880412588,

Delhi: 9891059875, **Nashik:** 9326967980, **Mumbai:** 9373440985

For accessing our unique 'System for Wisdom' from self-help to self-realization, please follow us on:

	Website	www.tejgyan.org
	Video Channel	www.youtube.com/tejgyan For Q&A videos: http://goo.gl/YA81DQ
	Social networking	www.facebook.com/tejgyan
	Social networking	www.twitter.com/sirshree
	Internet Radio	http://www.tejgyan.org internetradio.aspx

Online Shopping
www.gethappythoughts.org

Pray for World Peace along with thousands of others at 09:09 a.m. and p.m. every day

www.ingramcontent.com/pod-product-compliance
Lightning Source LLC
LaVergne TN
LVHW041705070526
838199LV00045B/1218